# Nonsenseorship

## G. G. Putnam

# Contents

# NONSENSEORSHIP

BY

G. G. Putnam

# WE HAVE WITH US TODAY

At current bootliquor quotations, Haig & Haig costs twelve dollars a quart, while any dependable booklegger can unearth a copy of "Jurgen" for about fifteen dollars. Which indicates, at least, an economic application of Nonsenseorship.

Its literary, social, and ethical reactions are rather more involved. To define them somewhat we invited a group of not-too-serious thinkers to set down their views regarding nonsenseorships in general and any pet prohibitions in particular.

In introducing those whose gems of protest are to be found in the setting of this volume, it is but sportsmanlike to state at the start that admission was offered to none of notable puritanical proclivity. The prohibitionists and censors are not represented. They require, in a levititious literary escapade like this, no spokesman. Their viewpoint already is amply set forth. Moreover, likely they would not be amusing.... Also, the exponents of Nonsenseorship are victorious; and at least the agonized cries of the vanquished, their cynical comment or outraged protest, should be given opportunity for expression!

Not that we consider HEYWOOD BROUN agonized, cynical, or outraged. Indeed, masquerading as a stalwart foe of inhibitions, he starts right out, at the very head of the parade, with a vehement advocacy of prohibition. His plea (surely, in this setting, traitorous) is to prohibit liquor to all who are over thirty years of age! He declares that "rum was designed for youthful days and is the animating influence which made oats wild." After thirty, presumably, Quaker Oats....

And at that we have quite brushed by GEORGE S. CHAPPELL. who serves a tasty appetizer at the very threshold, a bubbling cocktail of verse defining the authentic story of censorious gloom.

Censorship seems a species of spiritual flagellation to BEN HECHT, who, as he says, "ten years ago prided himself upon being as indigestible a type of the incoherent young as the land afforded." And nonsenseorship in general he regards as a war-born Frankenstein, a frenzied virtue grown hugely luminous; "a snowball rolling uphill toward God and gathering furious dimensions, it has escaped the shrewd janitors of orthodoxy who from age to age were able to keep it within bounds."

Then RUTH HALE, who visualizes glowing opportunities for feminine achievement in the functionings of inhibited society. "If the world outside the home is to become as circumscribed and paternalized as the world inside it, obviously all the advantage lies with those who have been living under nonsenseorship long enough to have learned to manage it."

WALLACE IRWIN is irrepressibly jocose (perhaps because he sailed for unprohibited England the day his manuscript was delivered), breaking into quite undisciplined verse anent the rosiness of life since the red light laws went blue.

"I am not sure, as I write, that this article ever will be printed," says ROBERT KEABLE, the English author of "Simon Called Peter." (It is). Mr. Keable, a minister from Africa, wrote of the war as he saw it in France, and in a way which offended people with mental blinders. He declares that the war quite completely knocked humbug on the head and bashed shams irreparably. "Rebels," says he, meaning those who speak their mind and write of things as they see them, "must be drowned in a babble of words."

And then HELEN BULLITT LOWRY, the exponent of the cocktailored young lady of today, averring that to the pocket-flask, that milepost between the time that was and the time that is, we owe the single standard of drinking. She maintains that the debutantalizing flapper, now driven right out in the open by the reformers, is the real salvation of our mid-victrolian society.

No palpitating defense of censorship would he expected from FREDERICK O'BRIEN of the South Seas, who contributes (and deliciously defines) a precious new word to the vocabulary of Nonsenseorship, "Wowzer." The nature of a wowzer is hinted in a ditty sung by certain uninhibited individuals as they lolled and imbibed among the mystic atolls and white shadows:

"Whack the cymbal! Bang the drum!
Votaries of Bacchus!

Let the popping corks resound,
Pass the flowing goblet round!
May no mournful voice be found,
Though wowzers do attack us!"

DOROTHY PARKER gives vent to a poignant Hymn of Hate, anent reformers, who "think everything but the Passion Play was written by Avery Hopwood," and whose dominant desire is to purge the sin from Cinema even though they die in the effort. "I hope to God they do," adds the author devoutly.

From England, through the eyes of FRANK SWINNERTON, we glimpse ourselves as others see us, and rather pathetically. In days gone by, lured by reports of America's lawless free-and-easiness, Swinnerton says he craved to visit us. But no more. The wish is dead. We have become hopelessly moral and uninviting. "I see that I shall after all have to live quietly in England with my pipe and my abstemious bottle of beer. And yet I should like to visit America, for it has suddenly become in my imagining an enormous country of 'Don't!' and I want to know what it is like to have 'Don't' said by somebody who is not a woman."

Also is raised the British voice of H. M. TOMLINSON, singed with satire. He writes as from a palely pure tomorrow when mankind shall have reached such a state of complete uniformity of soul, mind and body, that "only a particular inquiry will determine a man from a woman, though it may fail to determine a fool from a man." Tomlinson's imagined nation of the future is "as loyal and homogeneous, as contented, as stable, as a reef of actinozoal plasm." And over each hearth hangs the sacred Symbol--a portrait of a sheep.

Next is the usually jovial face of CHARLES HANSON TOWNE (that face which has launched a thousand quips) now all stern in his unbattled struggle with Prohibition, dourly surveying this "land of the spree and home of the grave."... "My children," says Towne, "as they sip their light wine and beer..." He is, at least, an optimist! But then, we are reminded he is also a bachelor.

In his own American language JOHN WEAVER pictures the feelings of an old-time saloon habitué when his former friend the barkeep, now rich from bootlegging, with a home "on the Drive" and all that, declares his socially-climbing daughter quite too good for this particular "Old Soak's" son. Weaver's retrospect of

"Bill's Place" will bring damp eyes to the unregenerate:

> "So neat! And over at the free-lunch counter,
> Charlie the coon with a apron white like chalk,
> Dishin' out hot-dogs, and them Boston Beans,
> And Sad'dy night a great big hot roast ham,
> Or roast beef simply yellin' to be et,
> And washed down with a seidel of Old Schlitz!"

"The Puritans disliked the theatre because it was jolly. It was a place where people went in deliberate quest of enjoyment." So says ALEXANDER WOOLLCOTT, who emerges as a sort of economic champion of stage morality, though no friend at all of censorship. Despite the *mot* "nothing risqué nothing gained," Woollcott emphatically declares the bed-ridden play is not, as a general thing, successful. "A blush is not, of course, a bad sign in the box-office," says he, developing his theme, "but the chuckle of recognition is better. So is the glow of sentiment, so is the tear of sympathy. The smutty and the scandalous are less valuable than homely humor, melodramatic excitement or pretty sentiment."

And last in this variegated and alphabeted company the anonymous AUTHOR OF "THE MIRRORS OF WASHINGTON" who views the applications of nonsenseorship from the standpoint of national politics.

G. P. P.

# EVOLUTION

### *Another of Those Outlines*

## BY GEORGE S. CHAPPELL

I

[*Time. The Beginning*.]

When Adam sat with lovely Eve
And. Pressed his Primal suit,  There was a ban, if we believe
Our Genesis, on fruit.  But did it give old Adam pause,
This One and only law there was?

X

[*Nine verses are supposed to elapse*.]

 And then great Moses, on the crest
Of Sinai, did devise  His tablets, acting for the best,
(Though some thought otherwise).  At least he showed restraint, for then
Man's sins were limited to *Ten*,

C

[*Ninety-nine verses elapse*.]

 In later days the Romans proud
Their famous Code began.  And lots of things were not allowed
By just Justinian.  He wrote a list, stupendous long;
*"One Hundred* Ways of Going Wrong."

M

[*Nine hundred and ninety-nine verses elapse.*]

Napoleon, (see Wells's book)
Improved the Roman plan  By spotting a potential crook
In every fellow-man.  And by the *Thousand* off they went
To jail, until proved innocent.

MDCCCCXXII

[*Nine thousand nine hundred and ninety-nine verses elapse.*]

Now in the change-about complete
Since Adam Passed from View.  For apples we are urged to eat
And all else is taboo.  A *Million* laws hold us in thrall,
And we serenely break them all!

# NONSENSEORSHIP
# HEYWOOD BROUN

A censor is a man who has read about Joshua and forgotten Canute. He believes that he can hold back the mighty traffic of life with a tin whistle and a raised right hand. For after all it is life with which he quarrels. Censorship is seldom greatly concerned with truth. Propriety is its worry and obviously impropriety was allowed to creep into the fundamental scheme of creation. It is perhaps a little unfortunate that no right-minded censor was present during the first week in which the world was made. The plan of sex, for instance, could have been suppressed effectively then and Mr. Sumner might have been spared the dreadful and dangerous ordeal of reading "Jurgen" so many centuries later.

Indeed, if there had only been right-minded supervision over the modelling of Adam and Eve the world could worry along nicely without the aid of the Society for the Suppression of Vice. Suppression of those biological facts which the Society includes in its definition of Vice is now impossible. Concealment is really what the good men are after. Somewhat after the manner of the Babes in the Woods they would cover us over with leaves. For men and women they have figs and for babies they have cabbages.

It must have been a censor who first hit upon the notion that what you don't know won't hurt you. We doubt whether it is a rule which applies to sex. Eve left Eden and took upon herself a curse for the sake of knowledge. It seems a little heedless of this heroism to advocate that we keep the curse and forget the knowledge. The battle against censorship should have ended at the moment of the eating of the apple. At that moment Man committed himself to the decision that he would know all about life even though he died for it. Unfortunately, under the terms of the existence of mortals one decision is not enough. We must keep reaffirming decisions if they are to hold. Even in Eden there was the germ of a new threat to degrade Adam and Eve back to innocence. When they ate the apple an amoeba in a distant corner of the Garden shuddered and began the long and difficult process of evolution. To all practical purposes John S. Sumner was already born.

To us the whole theory of censorship is immoral. If its functions were administered by the wisest man in the world it would still be wrong. But of course the wisest man in the world would have too much sense to be a censor. We are not dealing with him. His substitutes are distinctly lesser folk. They are not even trained for their work except in the most haphazard manner. Obviously a censor should be the most profound of psychologists. Instead the important posts in the agencies of suppression go to the boy who can capture the largest number of smutty post cards. After he has confiscated a few gross he is promoted to the task of watching over art. By that time he has been pretty thoroughly blasted for the sins of the people. An extraordinary number of things admit of shameful interpretations in his mind.

For instance, the sight of a woman making baby clothes is not generally considered a vicious spectacle in many communities, but it may not be shown on the screen in Pennsylvania by order of the state board of censors. In New York Kipling's Anne of Austria was not allowed to "take the wage of infamy and eat the bread of shame" in a screen version of "The Ballad of Fisher's Boarding House." Thereby a most immoral effect was created. Anne was shown wandering about quite casually and drinking and conversing with sailors who were perfect strangers to her, but the censors would not allow any stigma to be placed upon her conduct. Indeed this decision seems to support the rather strange theory that deeds don't matter so long as nothing is said about them.

The New York picture board is peculiarly sensitive to words. Upon one occasion a picture was submitted with the caption, "The air of the South Seas breathes an erotic perfume." "Cut out 'erotic,'" came back the command of the censors.

In Illinois, Charlie Chaplin was not allowed to have a scene in "The Kid" in which upon being asked the name of the child he shook his head and rushed into the house, returning a moment later to answer, "Bill." That particular board of censors seemed intent upon keeping secret the fact that there are two sexes.

Of course, it may be argued that motion pictures are not an art and that it makes little difference what happens to them. We cannot share that indifference. Enough has been done in pictures to convince us that very beautiful things might be achieved if only the censors could be put out of the way. Not all the silliness of the modern American picture is the fault of the producers. Much of the blame must rest with the various boards of censorship. It is difficult to think up many stories in which there is no passion, crime, or birth. As a matter of fact, we are of the opinion that the entire theory of motion picture censorship is mistaken. The guardians of morals hold that if the spectator sees a picture of a man robbing a safe he will thereby be moved to want to rob a safe himself. In rebuttal we offer the testimony of a gentleman much wiser in the knowledge of human conduct than any censor. Writing in "The New Republic," George Bernard Shaw advocated that hereafter public reading-rooms supply their patrons only with books about evil characters. For, he argued, after reading about evil deeds our longings for wickedness are satisfied vicariously. On the other hand there is the danger that the public may read about saints and heroes and drain off its aspirations in such directions without actions.

We believe this is true. We once saw a picture about a highwayman (that was in the days before censorship was as strict as it is now) and it convinced us that the profession would not suit us. We had not realized the amount of compulsory riding entailed. The particular highwayman whom we saw dined hurriedly, slept infrequently, and invariably had his boots on. Mostly he was being pursued and hurdling over hedges. It left us sore in every muscle to watch him. At the end of the eighth reel every bit of longing in our soul to be a swashbuckler had abated. The man in the picture had done the adventuring for us and we could return in comfort to a peaceful existence.

Florid literature is the compensation for humdrummery. If we are ever completely shut off from a chance to see or read about a little evil-doing we shall probably be moved to go out and cut loose on our own. So far we have not felt the necessity. We have been willing to let D'Artagnan do it.

Even so arduous an abstinence as prohibition may be made endurable through fictional substitutes. After listening to a drinking chorus in a comic opera and watching the amusing antics of the chief comedian who is ever so inebriated we are almost persuaded to stay dry. Prohibition is perhaps the climax of censorship. It has the advantage over other forms of suppression in that at least it represents a sensible point of view. Yet, we are not converted. There are things in the world far more important than hard sense.

One of the officials of the Anti-Saloon League gave out a statement the other day in which he endeavored to show all the benefits provided by prohibition. But he did it with figures. There was a column showing the increase of accounts in savings banks and another devoted to the decrease of inmates in hospitals, jails and almshouses. From a utilitarian point of view the figures, if correct, could hardly fail to be impressive, but little has been said by either side about the spiritual aspects of rum. Unfortunately there are no statistics on that, and yet it is the one phase of the question which interests us. Some weeks ago we happened to observe a letter from a man who wrote to one of the newspapers protesting against the proposed settlement in Ireland on the ground that, "It's so damned sensible." We have somewhat the same feeling about prohibition. It is a movement to take the folly out of our national life and there is no quality which America needs so sorely.

If enforcement ever becomes perfect this will be a nation composed entirely of men who wear rubbers, put money in the bank, and go to bed at ten. That fine old ringing phrase, "This is on me," will be gone from the language. Conversation will be wholly instructive, for in fifty years the last generation capable of saying, "Do you remember that night--?" will have been gathered to its fathers.

Of course, there is no denying the shortsightedness of the forces of rum. They cannot escape their responsibility for having aided in the advent of Prohibition. They were slow to see the necessity of some form of curtailment and limitation of the traffic. Such moves as they did make were entirely wrong-headed. For instance, we had ordinances providing for the early closing of cafés. Instead of that we should have had laws forbidding anybody to sell liquor except between the hours of 8 P.M. and 5 A.M. Daytime drinking was always sodden, but something is necessary to make night worth while. Man is more than the beasts, and he should not be driven into dull slumber just because the sun has set.

The invention of electricity, liquor, cut glass mirrors, and cards made man the master of his environment rather than its slave. Now that liquor is gone all the other factors are mockery. Card playing has become merely an extension of the cruel and logical process of the survival of the fittest. The fellow with the best hand wins, instead of the one with the best head. Nobody draws four cards any more or stands for a raise on an inside straight. The thing is just cut-throat and scientific and wholly mercenary.

The kitty is gone. Nobody cares to come in to a common fund for the purchase of mineral water and cheese sandwiches. And with the passing of the kitty the most promising development of co-operation and communism in America has gone. It was prophetic of a more perfectly organized society. In the days of the kitty the fine Socialistic ideal of, "From each according to his abilities; to each according to his needs," was made specific and workable. And the inspiring romantic tradition of Robin Hood was also carried over into modern life. The kitty robbed only the rich and left the poor alone.

But now none of us will contribute unquestionably to the material comfort of others. Each must keep his money for the savings bank.

Perhaps, something of the old friendly rivalry may be revived. In a hundred years it may be that men will meet around a table and that one will say to the other, "What have you got?"

"I've got $9,876.32 in first mortgages and gilt-edged securities."

"That's good. You win."

But somehow or other we doubt it.

Another mistake which was made in the policy of compromising with the drys was the agreement that liquor should not be served to minors. On the contrary, the provision should have been that drink ought not to be permitted to any man more than thirty years of age. Liquor was never meant to be a steady companion. It was the animating influence which made oats wild. Work and responsibility are the portion of the mature man. Rum was designed for youthful days when the reckless avidity for experience is so great that reality must be blurred a little lest it blind us.

We happened to pick up a copy of "The Harvard Crimson" the other day and read: "The first freshman smoker will be held at 7.45 o'clock this evening in the living room of the Union. P. H. Theopold, '25, Chairman of the Smoker Committee, will act as Chairman, introducing Clark Hodder, '25, and J. H. Child, '25, the Class President and Secretary respectively. After the speeches there will be a motion picture, and some vaudeville by a magician from Keith's. Ginger ale, crackers, and cigarettes will be served. All freshmen are invited to attend."

They used to be called Freshmen Beer Nights and in those days the possibility of friendship at first sight was not fantastic. We feel sure that it cannot be done on ginger ale. The urge for democracy does not dwell in any soft drink. The speeches will be terrible, for there will be no pleasant interruptions of "Aw, sit down," from the man in the back of the room. If somebody begins to sing, "P. H. Theopold is a good old soul," it is not likely to carry conviction. Not once during the evening will any speaker confine himself to saying, "To Hell with Yale!" and falling off the table. Probably the magician will not be able to find anything in the high hat except white rabbits.

Although we have seen no first hand report of that freshman smoker, we feel sure that it was only a crowded self-conscious gathering of a number of young men who said little and went home early.

Even from the standpoint of the strictest of abstainers there must be some re-gret for the passing of rum. What man who lived through the bad old days does not remember the thrill of rectitude which came to him the first time he said, "Make mine a cigar."

Though they have taken away our rum from us we have our memories. Not all the days have been dull gray. Back in the early pages of our diary is the entry about the trip which we made to Boston with William F---- in the hard winter of 1907. It was agreed that neither of us should drink the same sort of drink twice. Staunch William achieved nineteen varieties, but we topped him with twenty-four. Upon examination we observe that the entry in the memory book was made several days later. The handwriting is a little shaky. But for that adventure we might have lived and died entirely ignorant of the nature of an Angel Float.

In those days human sympathy was wider. F. M. W. seemed in many respects a matter-of-fact man, but it was he who chanced upon the 59th street Circle just before dawn and paused to call the attention of all bystanders to the statue of Co-lumbus.

"Look at him," he said. "Christopher Columbus! He discovered America and then they sent him back to Spain in chains."

He wept, and we realized for the first time that under a rough exterior there beat a heart of gold.

# LITERATURE AND THE BASTINADO
## BEN HECHT

Surveying the trend of modern literature one must, unless one's mental processes be complicated with opaque prejudices, wonder at the provoking laxity of the national censorship. I write from the viewpoint of an aggrieved iconoclast.

It becomes yearly more obvious that the duly elected, commissioned and delegated high priests of the nation's morale are growing blind to the dangers which assail them. If not, then how does it come that such enemies of the public weal as H. L. Mencken, Floyd Dell, Sherwood Anderson, Theodore Dreiser, Dos Passos, Mr. Cabell, Mr. Rascoe, Mr. Sandburg, Mr. Sinclair Lewis are not in jail? How does it come Professor Frinck of Cornell is not in jail? Bodenheim, Margaret Anderson, Mr. John Weaver are not in jail.

Were I the President of the United States sworn to uphold the dignity of its psychopathic repressions, pledged on a stack of Bibles to promote the relentless pursuit and annihilation of other people's happiness, I would have begun my reign by clapping H. L. Mencken into irons forthwith. Mr. Cabell, I would have sent to Russia. Sherwood Anderson I would have boiled in oil.

But what is the situation? Observe these gentlemen and their kin enjoying not only their bodily liberty but allowed to prosper on the royalties derived from the sale of incendiary volumes designed to destroy the principles upon which the integrity of the commonwealth depends. The spectacle is one aggravating to an iconoclast. There is no affront as distressing as the tolerance of one's enemies.

Mr. H. L. Mencken is, perhaps, the outstanding victim of this depravity of indifference which more and more characterizes the enemy. Mr. Mencken, hurling himself for ten years against the Bugaboo of Puritanism--a fearless and wonderfully caparisoned Knight of Alarums, Prince of Darkness, Evangel of Chaos--Mr. Mencken pauses for a moment out of breath casting about slyly for fresher and deadlier weapons and lo! the Bugaboo with a gentle smile reaches out and embraces him and plants the kiss of love on both his cheeks, strokes his hair wistfully, and invites him to sit on the front porch. Alas, poor Mencken! It is the fate that awaits us all. Zarathustra in the market-place feeding ground glass to the populace is gathered to the bosom of the City Fathers and gleefully enrolled as a member of the Guild.

This is no idle rhetoric. Dissent in the Republic has come upon hard ways. Ten years ago the name of Mencken would have stood against the world. Today no college freshman, no lowly professor, no charity worker, or local alderman too puritanical to do him homage.

Whereupon the argument is that an era of enlightenment has set in, that this same Mencken and his contemporary throat-cutters have vanquished the Bugaboo, and that, as a result, a spirit of high intellectual life prevails through the land. The proletaire have risen and are thumbing their nose at the gods. Brander Matthews has sent in a five years' subscription to the Little Review. The Comstocks overcome with the vision of their ghastly complexes are appealing to Sigmund Freud for advice and relief. But the argument is superficial. "Victory!" cry the iconoclasts grinding their teeth at the absence of a foe.

But it is a victory that rankles in the soul. The foe is not vanquished but, seemingly, bored to death has fallen asleep. It is, in any event, a phenomenon. Many generalizations offer themselves as solace.

The first paradox of this phenomenon is that Puritanism, beaten to a pulp by an ever-increasing herd of first, second, third, and fourth rate iconoclasts, has triumphed completely in the legislatures of the country. With every new volume exposing the gruesome mainsprings of the national virtue, further taboos and restrictions crowd themselves into the statute books.

In a sense it would seem as if the ***bete populaire***, becoming increasingly drunk with the consciousness of its own power, is elatedly preoccupied in cutting off its own nose, tying itself up into knots, and kicking itself in the rear, proclaiming simultaneously and in triumphant tones, "Observe how powerful I am. I can pass laws making ipecac a compulsory diet."

Whereupon the laws are passed and the noble masses with heroic grimaces fall to devouring ipecac, to the confusion of all free-born stomachs. In fact this species of ballot flagellatism, this diverting pastime of hitting itself on the head with a stuffed club has gradually elevated the body politic to the enviable position occupied by the all-powerful king of Fernando Po. This mysterious being lives in the lowest depths of the crater of Riabba. His power is in direct ratio to the taboos which hem him in. Convinced that bathing is a crime against his dignity, that sunlight is incompatible with his royal lineage; convinced that his prestige is dependent upon a weekly three days' fast and a cautious observation of the taboos against all variants of social inter-course--piously convinced of these astounding things, the all-powerful monarch of Fernando Po sits year in and year out motionless on his throne in the lowest depths of the crater of Riabba, awed by himself and overcome with the contemplation of his all-powerfulness. We have here, I trust, an illuminating analogy.

The Republic, like this King of Fernando Po, imposes daily upon itself new taboos, new rituals. Yet there is the phenomenon of its tolerance toward the idol breakers. From the lowest depths of the crater of Riabba in which he sits enthroned the monarch of the Laongos condemns to death with a twitch of his brows all who seek to question the sanctity of the taboos. But this other occupant of the crater of Riabba-our Republic-raises gentle eyes to the idol wreckers, to the taboo destroy-ers. An occasional, "tut tut" escapes him. And nothing more.

Whereupon the argument is that our monarch of the pit is an impotent fellow. Again, a superficial deduction. For behold the censorships with which he belabors himself.

Censorship, almost extinct in the restriction of the national literature, thrives in every other field. Censorships abound. Food, drink, movies, politics, baseball, di-version, dress--all these are under the jurisdiction of a continually aroused censor-ship. The pulpits and editorial pages emit sonorous hymns of taboo. Every caption writer is an Isaiah, every welfare worker fancies himself the handwriting on the wall. Unchallenged by the vote of the masses or by any outward evidence of mass dissent, the platitudes pile up, the nation is filled from morning to morning with stentorian clamor. Puritanism in a frenetic finale approaches a climax.

But, and we tiptoe towards the crux of this phenomenon, the Bacchanal of Presbyterianism is an artificial climax. Unlike the day of the later Caesars, the popu-lace does not abandon itself in imitation of its Neros and Caligulas. Instead, we have the spectacle of a populace apathetic toward the spirit of its time.

The Puritan debauch is the logical culmination of the anti-Paganism and back-worldism launched two hundred centuries back. The Christian ethic, to the bewildered chagrin of its advocates, has triumphed. Not a triumph this time that offers itself as a cloak for Jesuitism, colonization, or empire juggling. But an unimpeachable triumph entirely beyond the control of the most adroit of the choir-Machiavellis.

In other words the body politic finds itself betrayed by its own platitudes. A moral frenzy animates its horizon. But it is a frenzy of idea escaped control, an idea grown too huge and luminous to direct any longer. The moral frenzy of the war was the moral frenzy of such an idea--virtue become a Frankenstein. This virtue--the Golden Rule, the Thou Shalt Nots, the thousand and one unassailable maxims, adages, old saws invented chiefly for the protection of the weak and the solace of the inferior--this virtue has taken itself out of the hands of its hitherto adroit worshippers. A snowball rolling uphill toward God and gathering furious dimensions, it has escaped the shrewd janitors of orthodoxy who from age to age were able to keep it within bounds.

Thus in the war, confronted with the platitude that the world must be made safe for democracy and with the further platitude that democracy and equality were the goals of Christianity and with a dozen similar platitudes none of which had any authentic contact with the life of the nation, thus confronted, the proletaire was forced to lift itself up by its boot straps and rise to the defence of a Frankenstein idealism of which it was the parent-victim. Disillusionment with the causes of the war has, however, served no high purpose. The Frankenstein God, the Frankenstein virtue is still enshrined in the Heaven of the Copy Books. And we find the proletaire still worshipping, albeit with the squirmings and grimacings, a horrible idealization of itself.

The Thou Shalt Nots have escaped. They increase and multiply with a life of their own. Logic is the most irresponsible of the manias which operate in life. Logic demands that ideas be carried to their climax and this demand, as inexorable as Mr. Newton's law, has made a Frankenstein of the unsuspecting Galilean.

Hypnotized by the demands of logic, bewildered by the contemplation of this code of backworldism which he himself seems somehow to have created, the ballot maniac stands riveted at the polls and sacrifices to his own image by hitting himself on the head with further virtuous restrictions--a gesture necessary to prevent his own image from giving him the lie. He must, in other words, prove himself as virtuous, whenever public demonstration demands, as the Frankenstein platitudes proclaim him to be.

The Puritanism of the nation, remorselessly upheld by its laws and its public factotums is an extraneous and artificial pose into which the blundering proletaire has tricked itself. There are innumerable consequences. We have, firstly, the spectacle of the masses disporting themselves slyly in the undertow of cynicism.

"Modesty," bellows Sir Frankenstein from pulpit and press, "is a cardinal virtue." "Right O," echoes the feminine contingent and promptly bobs its hair, shortens its skirts, and rolls down its socks.

"Abstinence, sobriety, are an economic and spiritual necessity," bellows Sir Frankenstein. Whereupon the male contingent votes the land dry and gets drunk.

From the foregoing we may derive glimmers of truth concerning the public tolerance of iconoclasts. "Main Street," a volume fathered by Mencken, Freud, and the other Chaos-Bringers, leaps into prominence as a best seller. It is devoured and acclaimed by the ballot maniac who reads it, smacks his lips over its "truths" and sallies forth to vote further canonizations of hypocrisy into the legal code. Even I, who ten years ago prided myself upon being as indigestible a type of the Incoherent Young as the land afforded, find myself for one month a best seller[1] on my native heath. Woe the prophet who is with honor in his country! He will flee in disgust in quest of hair shirts and a bastinado.

Thus, the citizens. With the left hand they greet the iconoclasts and hand them royalties. With the right hand they pass further laws for the iconoclasts to denounce. A phenomenon results. With the thought of the masses becoming more and more neutral in the highty-tighty war between Good and Evil, the laws created by these same masses grow more and more rabid. But it must be borne in mind that although the masses, carried away by flagellant impulses, assist in the creation of these laws, in the main, they are laws, self-created platitudes which give birth to new platitudes. Logic is the most pernicious of the Holy Ghosts responsible for the conception of undesirable Gods.

I am prepared now to make further revelations. The foregoing, although bris-

---

1   "Erik Dorn," Mr. Hecht's first novel.--Ed.

tling with inconsistencies, seems to me, nevertheless, a ground work. I will begin the apocalyptic finale with a resume of the choir-leaders, the high priests, the Mahatmas of Sir Frankenstein.

Item one: It is obvious that the laws of the land being the ghastly climaxes of artificial logic and not of human desires or biological necessities, therefore the salaried apostles of these laws must function similarly outside nature.

The high priests, it develops indeed upon investigation, diligently lickspittling to Sir Frankenstein, have no following. The masses are not going to Heaven in their wake. They, the high priests, are magically out of touch with their worshippers. And from day to day they grow further out of touch until they are to be seen high in the clouds tending the fugitive altars that are soaring toward God on their own power.

These high priests are the creatures elected, commissioned and delegated by the proletaire to perpetuate its grandiose and impossible image. And this they do. They are the custodians of the public morals, meaning the protectors of the huge trick mirror out of which the complexes, neurasthenias, and morbid fears of the public stare back at it in the guise of Virtue, Honor, Decency, and Love. These custodians are also, to leap into the denouement, the censors here under discussion; censors not only tolerated but insisted upon by the people to annoy and harass them and inspire them to further ballot flagellations in order that they, the people, may be spared the disaster of discovering themselves different from what two hundred centuries of self-idealization have driven them into believing themselves to be.

This, the high priests do. In every village, hamlet and farm they have their say. They chastise. They make things fit for decent people to see or wear or drink, and people flattered to death at the idea of being considered decent submit piously to the distastement infringements and taboos.

All-powerful are the censors. But despite this all-powerfulness they labor under a wretched handicap. They are stupid. Stupidity is the paradox to be found most often in all-powerful Gods. They are stupid, the censors. And the Devil is clever. The Seven Arts which are the Seven Incarnations of Dionysius, the Seven Masks of an unrepentant Lucifer, elude them in the horrific struggle. Or at least partially elude them. Occasionally a cloven hoof is spied and sliced to the bone.

\*      \*      \*      \*      \*

We return now with proud and tranquil ease to the beginning of this tale, to the phenomenon of a tolerated literary iconoclasm in a land alive with caterwaulings of virtue.

As hinted above not all the Arts escape, nor do any of them escape all the time. Music, whose sly and terrible vices were for centuries unperceived by the high priests, has been brought to earth in places. "Jazz Incites to Sin. Syncopation is Devil's Ally." Discovered! One reads the morning paper and feels a return of hope. The High Priests are aroused. They have disembowelled an ally. There is hope then of a bloody fray. Another Edition and they will be on our own heads, swinging their snickersnees. Mencken will be arrested and burned in public. Anderson will be strung up by the heels and his estates confiscated. There will be war--red war, and we in the army of the iconoclasts growling impotently at each other will face about and have at them with hullaballo and manifesto and snickersnee in turn.

"Nude Painting Banned From Window. Nab Store Keeper." We read on. The snickersnee swings towards the vitals of Hollywood. "Movie Magnate Charges Work of Art Cut; Sues Censors. Seeks Redress in Courts."

Valhalla! They are closing in. Another forced march and they are upon us.

Alas, our coffee cools as we wait impatiently for the alarms to sound. We are intact. Mencken still lives. Anderson still lives. The tide of battle sweeps us by, passes us up, and there's the end to it.

Again, our victory rankling, we cast about for reasons. Do not the censors read our books? Yes, the censors read our books. And scratching their necks pensively and immediately below their left ears, the censors fall asleep. Our books were over their heads. Our broadsides aimed for their vitals whizzed by their ears and lulled them into slumber. A hideous victory is in our hands.

Voltaire blew God out of France for a century. But that was because God was still an emotion in his day and not a Frankenstein of logic. He blew up the high priests. But that was because the high priests still had enough intelligence in that time to know what constituted an epoch-shaking explosion.

Our enemies the censors, the hallelujah flingers, commissioned, elected, delegated by the proletaire are not worthy our steel. Having no longer any contact with the masses, they need no genius to perpetuate themselves. The masses care not what they are so long as they are. Figureheads for Frankenstein, they need only shriek themselves blue and their will, will be done. Shrewdness, intelligence, are qualities non-essential since virtue, no longer feeding upon shrewdness and intelligence, fattens upon its own monstrous logic.

The high priests are vital to the lie which man has created for himself as a heaven and out of which his own image leers godlike back at him. They are vital for nothing else.

Therefore our immunity. Since they need no grey matter, they have none. And unable to understand us, they ignore us. And if we grow too insistent, as has Mencken, they put an end to the business by embracing us and pulling our fangs by disgusting us with their stupidity.

Given free reign under the conditions herein outlined, the youth of the land is abandoning itself to a safe and sane orgie of iconoclasm. Satanic epigrams cloud the air of the very market-place. Poets, column conductors, hack literary reviewers, hack romancers, lecturers, realists, imagists, and all are gloatingly engaged in sacking the Temple, in thumbing their nose at the taboos.

In fact so widespread is the unlicensed and unrebuked iconoclasm of the day that a great disgust is being born in the hearts of the pioneers. Every dog has his paradox, every hack his anti-Christ, they bewail. And surveying the horizon despairingly they see no enemy rushing upon them with the wind.

There are, of course, scattered here and there among the keepers of the Seal, observant priests. They omit isolated groans. They launch Quixotic sorties. But they retire and collapse without waiting combat. To their denunciation of "degenerate, sinful and corrupting cesspools of alleged art" (I quote from a review of some of my own work appearing in an issue of the Springfield (Ill.) ***Republican***), there is no answering response. They are left abandoned, the Fiery Cross burning down to their fingers and flickering out. They cannot be glorified into an enemy.

On the whole I fear for the result. Ideas favor a bloody battle-ground for birthplace. And here we stand, drawn up in battle array discharging broadsides of "Winesburgs, Ohios," "Main Streets," "Cornhuskers" and the like; flying our colors valiantly--but there is no battle. The enemy sleeps. Or the enemy wakes up and issues an indifferent invitation that we stay to tea.

Comrade Dreiser may demur at all this and, peeling his vest, reveal us wounds, honorable wounds acquired in honorable battle. And further, he may regale us with tales of hair shirts and bastinadoes suffered by him in the Republic. But alas, he is Telemachus, grey-bearded and full of memories. And the youth of Athens, fallen upon softer ways, listen with envious incredulity to such tall tales.

# THE WOMAN'S PLACE
# RUTH HALE

At last the women of this country are about to perform a great service--not one of those courtesy services about which so much is so volubly said and so little is done in repayment--but a good sturdy performance, that will probably bring these magnificent men folks right to their knees. They are going to teach the unfortunates how to live under prohibitions and taboos. Of course there has never been any prodigality of freedom in this country--or any other--but what there was belonged to the men. The women had to take to the home and stay there. So the two sexes adjusted themselves to life with this difference, that the women had to do all the outwitting and circumventing, all the little smart twists and turns, all the cunning scheming by which people snatch off what they want without appearing to, whereas men got their much or little by prosily sticking their hands out for it.

This developed, naturally, not only somewhat diverse temperaments, hut also greatly diverse equipments. When men cannot get what they want now by either asking or paying for it, they have no more resources. Bless them, they must return into the home, where the secret has been perfected for centuries on centuries of how to hoard a private stock and how to find a bootlegger. Under the steadily growing nonsenseorship regime, they are obliged to come and take lessons from the lately despised group of creatures to whom nonsenseorship is a well-thumbed story. If the world outside the home is to become as circumscribed and paternalized as the world inside it, obviously all the advantage lies with those who have been living under nonsenseorship long enough to have learned to manage it.

Thus woman moves over from her dull post as keeper of the virtues to the far more important and exciting post as keeper of the vices. It is not an ideal power which she thus acquires. But then none of this is about ideals. This is just a little practical 'study in what is going to happen, and why. Taboos never yet have added a cubit to the stature of the soul of humanity. They have nearly always been the chattering children of fear and pure idiocy. They have always tried to throw the race back on to all fours, and have left the nobility of standing upright wholly out of account.

The taboos which have surrounded women time out of mind have been so puerile and imbecile that one quite non-partisanly wonders why on earth they have been allowed to continue. A second thought demonstrates, of course, that fear has had the major part in it, and that skill in cheating has gone so far as practically to nullify the privations of the taboo.

But one must put by this hankering after nobility, and accept the plain fact that fear is the dominant human motive. What the race would do if fear were conquered, or at least faced sternly eye to eye, is staggering to contemplate. Perhaps God looks upon that vision. It may be that which gives Him patience. But man at best gives it one terrified squint in a lifetime. All behavior must take fear into account.

The man who lately brought back from the Amazon Basin news of a fear-dispelling drug used there by a savage tribe, would have been carried home from the steamer on the shoulders of his compatriots if for one moment he had been believed. His drug may do all he claimed for it, but a country which boasts a Volstead in full stride cannot force itself to take him seriously. The only likely part of his story was that the tribes who prepared the drug would put to instant death any woman who happened either to learn how to prepare it or did actually get some of it into her.

We recognize that part as familiar. We have made the same fight here against the fearless woman as the savages made on the Amazon. The only thing we were never smart enough to apply was the moral of the Kipling story about the two greatest armies in the world: the men who believed that they could not die till their time came, against those who wanted to die as soon as possible. It was from one or the other of these two kinds of fearlessness that women have trained themselves in wisdom. This is the wisdom which moves them to secret laughter when they find their brothers in the throes of Volstead and Krafts. And it is from this wisdom that they will teach them all to be happy, though prohibited.

It is an unfortunate fact that humanity will not behave itself. It does not really warm to any of the current virtues. When the Eighteenth Amendment says it must not drink hard liquors, its inner heart's desire is to drink them, even beyond its normal, and usual capacity. Prohibition is, it is true, one of the strikingly superimposed virtues. It has nothing whatever to recommend it in man's true feelings, and this is not true of many of the civilized traits, though probably not any of them meets with entire approval. We do think that before anything approaching a real art of living is perfected among us, the present ethical system will be wholly outmoded. Meanwhile, pressure brought to bear on the least welcome of all virtues is merely going to make bad behavior worse. But that is Volstead's business, not ours. Let him do battle with that octopus, while we bring up reinforcements to his enemies. Women know all about how to be bad and comfortable while the law goes on trying to make them good and otherwise. Just look at a few of the things on which they have cut their teeth.

We do not know, unfortunately, just at what point in her history woman went under the long siege of her taboos. Whether the system of keeping her publicly helpless and interdicted goes before church and state, or was the result of them, there is now no history to tell us. But certainly she always had one supreme power and one supreme weakness, and somewhere in time, her more neutrally equipped male companion played the one against her, to save his own skin from being stripped by the other.

But if the past is foggy, the present is not. We do know what is now, and has for a long time been, a shocking list of what she must not be allowed to do.

She cannot own and control her own property, for instance, except here and there in the world. Perhaps the theory was that she could not create property. But one would have said that such of it as she inherited she had as sound a right to as that that her brother inherited. But no such common sense notion prevailed. No matter how she came by it, it became her husband's as soon as she married. The law has always behaved as if a woman became a half-wit the moment she married. Seeing what she deliberately lost by it, perhaps the law is right. She lost control of her possessions, including herself. She lost her citizenship, and she lost her name, though this by custom and not by law. And finally, she never could acquire control even over her own children, which certainly she did create. We do not know how many of these disabilities would have been excused on the ground that they were for her own good. It seems likelier that they came under the head of that fine old abstraction, the general good. No longer back than 1914, H. G. Wells, in "Social Forces in England and America" observed that they would probably never be able to give women any real freedom because there were the children to consider. Mr. Wells did not appear to know that he was bridging a horrible conflict in terms with a pretty fatuity. Nor did he later give himself pause when, towards the end of the book, he complained that all the babies were being had by the low grade women, while the high grade ones were quite insensible to their duties.

It was possibly with an unruliness of this kind in contemplation that the law decided that women should know nothing of birth control. Now there's a taboo for you. Many of our very best people--the moral element, so called--will not even speak the words. But that prohibition, like all the others, has its side door--may one say its small-family entrance? The women who do not know all there is to know about it are just those poor, isolated, and ignorant women economically starved who should be the first to be told.

Consider the quaintest, we think, of all the proscriptions against women--that they cannot have citizenship in their own right. What is citizenship if it is not the assumption, made by the State, that because you were born within it, and had grown used to it and fond of it, and were attached to it by all the associations of blood ties, friendships, and what not, you were therefore entitled to take part in it, and could be called on to give it service? If citizenship is a mere legal figment, by what right do States send their citizens to war? Yet women are theoretically transferred, body and bone, heart, memory, and soul, to whatever country or nation their husbands happen to give allegiance to. Isadora Duncan, born in California, of generations of Californians, and American all her life, has lately married a young Russian poet. Hereafter she must enter her country as an alien immigrant--if it so happens that the quota is not closed. Does anybody in his senses imagine that Isadora Duncan has been changed, or could be changed, for better or worse? An opera singer who was in danger during the war of losing her position at the Metropolitan Opera House because she was an enemy alien, went forth and married an American. By that means she was actually supposed to have been made over into an American. Can naïveté go further?

For our present purposes we merely want to point out that what is done to one woman in the name of the public good is craftily used by the next one to serve her own ends. There is a terrifying proportion of women in America today who can vote, without knowing a word of our language, without participating in one particle of our common life, because their husbands have taken on American citizenship. They wouldn't be allowed to become American citizens if they wanted to, by any other means.

There are scores and scores of these legal absurdities conscripting the activities of women. Twenty books could be written about them, and probably will be. But we must leave them, with such representation as these few instances afford, and go from, the body of taboos that are done in the name of the good of the State, to that collection done for Woman's own personal good.

Some of these are legal and some are not, but they are all operative. They are all things she has to go around, or under. She cannot serve on juries. She is always righteously barred from courtrooms when there is to be testimony concerning sex. Woman, the mother of children, the realist of sex compared to whom the most sympathetic of males is at best an outsider, is to be "protected" from a few scandalous narratives. Of course all women know that they are barred from juries not because the happenings in court would shock or even surprise them, but because they would embarrass their far more sensitive and finicky men. So what they wish to know of court proceedings, they learn from their good men, in the pleasant privacy of their homes. If the juries are so much the worse for this sort of thing, and they are, the matter cannot be helped by the ladies, dear knows, and the men would die almost any death liefer than that of ravaged modesty.

Probably the most ungrateful of the restrictions on females is that forbidding them to hold office in churches. This has been put on all sorts of high grounds, chief among them being that women could do so much abler work in little auxiliaries of their own. This contention was challenged about two years ago in the House of Commons, by Maud Royden, the English Lay Evangelist to whom the pulpits of London are forbidden, with one or two exceptions. Miss Royden, whose preaching was being bitterly opposed by several members of the House, annoyed them all considerably by saying that the Church of England had already had two women as its absolute head. This was denied in a great sputter, to which Miss Royden replied, "How about Queen Elizabeth and Queen Victoria?" Well, this happened to be something that nobody could gainsay, but into the wrathy silence which followed, one member of the House rose to his feet and let the cat right out of the bag. If women were given church authority, he said, they would refuse to accept their husbands' authority in their homes, and England would go to rack and ruin. This is one of the few recorded occasions when a taboo-er so far forgot himself, and American church potentates do not like to be reminded of it. Within a month, one of the Protestant sects in this country has given women the right to hold minor offices, but three others, in general convention, refused even to consider it.

Again we are going to rest our case on selected instances, and return to a consideration of how these walled-in women have learned to live comfortably and with some self-respect behind the garrison wall. It is this, after all, which they must now teach their men.

The first thing that happened to the woman who married was that she became legally non-existent. But though she was scratched off the public books, she couldn't exactly be scratched out of her husband's scheme of general well-being. Neither could the race make great strides without her. After everything in the world had been done to make her as harmless as possible, she still remained non-ignorable. Two courses were open to her; and she has always used whichever of the two was necessary at the time. She could be so sweet and beguiling, so full of blandishments, that man rushed out to bring her all and more than she had been prohibited from having. Or she could terrify him, both by her temper and her biological superiority, into stopping his entire precious machinery against her, and thanking his stars that he could get off with a whole skin.

Of course these things have not always worked out just so. There have been the tragic mischances. But in the main, an oppressed people learn how to outsmile or outsnarl the oppressor. The Eighteenth Amendment may yet live to wish it was dead. Mr. Volstead seems to have believed that the nonsenseorship game was new and exciting, and could be trusted to carry itself by storm. Not while the ancient wisdom of long-borne bans and communicadoes looked out of the female eye. There was a body of experts in existence of whom, apparently, he had never even heard.

He never once thought how the twentieth century was to become known as the Century of The Home, with the home brew, and the subscription editions, and the sagacities of women. If he should complain that there is no honor and fine living in all of this, we shall have to agree with him. But we can answer that by guile we have preserved our joys, and cleared our way out from the shadows of his big totem pole. If we have but little magnificence, we have as much as anybody can ever have who is hounded by the legal virtues. And if we may keep a little gaiety for life, by that much do we make him bite the dust. It isn't pretty, but it's art.

# OWED TO VOLSTEAD
# WALLACE IRWIN

I--*First Round*

Prune extract and bright alcohol, so wooden
One kills its flavor in rank fusel oil!
C2-H3-HO--a rather good 'un
To mix with fruity syrups in our toil
To give our social meetings after dark
Their necessary spark!
And you, most heavenly twins,
Born of one mother--
Although our woe begins
When, through our mortal sins,
We can't tell which from 'tother--
Ethyl
And Methyl!
Like Ike
And Mike
Strangely you look alike.
Like sisters I have met
You're very hard to tell apart--and yet
The one consoles more gently than a wife;
The other turns and cripples you for life.

Such spirits as these, and many more I summon
From many a poisoned tin,
Or many a bottle falsely labelled "Gin."
Or many a vial pathetic,
Yclept "Synthetic."
Like Dante on his joy-ride Seeing Hell,
Fain would I take you down
Through sulphurous fires and caverns bilious brown
Into the Land of Mystery and Smell
Where Satan steweth
And home-breweth
While thirsty hooch-hounds yell
Their blackest curse,
Or worse:
"Vol-darn our souls with each Vol-blasted dram
That burns our throats and isn't worth a dam!
We drink, yet how we dread it--
Vol-stead it!"
They've said it.


## II--*Short Intermission to Change Meter*

In Eighteen Hundred and Sixty-three
A. Lincoln set the darkies free;
In Nineteen Hundred and Nineteen
A. Volstead muzzled the canteen
And freed the millions, great and small,
From bondage to King Alcohol.

Was it not thoughtful, good and kind
For such a man of such a mind
To show an interest so grand

In his misguided native land?
And don't these statements illustrate
Our Nation's progress up to date?
We're freedom-loving and we're brave
And simply cannot stand a slave.
And when a crisis needs a man
From Mass, or Tex. or Conn, or Kan.
That man steps forward, firm of chin--
So Andrew Volstead came from Minn.

He came from Minn, to show the world
That gin is wrong
And rye is strong
And Scotch to limbo should be hurled.
Thus with his spotless flag unfurled
He went against the Demon Rum
Who snarled, "I vum!"
Got sort of numb,
Rolled up his eyes, lay down and curled
While all the saints of heaven above
(Including Mr. Bryan's Dove)
Cried "Rah-rah-rah!
And siss-boom-ah!
Three cheers for Health and Christian Love!
But, Andrew dear--
Say, now, look here!
You're not including wine and beer!"

Then Andrew Volstead squared his chin
And answered briefly, "Sin is sin."
No compromise
With the King of Lies!
Both liquor thick and liquor thin

We'll cease to tax
And use the axe
Invented by the Man from Minn.
For right is right and wrong is wrong--
A spell has cursed the world too long.

The curse of drink--
Stop, friends, and think
How, reft of spirits weak or strong,
My Nation will be purified
Of all corruptions vile.
The lamb and lion, side by side,
Will smile and smile and smile.
The workman when his day is o'er
Will hurry to his cottage door
To kiss his loving wife;
He'll lay his wages in her hand
And peace will settle on the land
Without a trace of strife.
The criminals will cease to swarm,
Forgers and burglars will reform
And minor crimes will so abate
That lower courts--now open late--
Will close and let the magistrate
Go to the zoo
Or read **Who's Who**.
In short I do anticipate
A thinner, cooler human race,
Its system cleansed of every trace
Of inner fire
And hot desire
And passions spurring to disgrace.
"'Tis simple," said the Man from Minn.,

"To cure the world of mortal sin--
Just legislate against it."
Then up spake Congress with a roar,
"We never thought of that before.
Let's go!"
And they commenced it.


III-- *Tone Picture's Suggesting Conditions in U. S. A. Some Two Years After Alcoholic Stimulants Had Been Legislated out of Business*

1
Grandma's sitting in her attic,
Oiling up her automatic.
Mid-Victorian is her style,
Prim yet gentle is her smile
As she fits the cartridges
One by one, and softly says:

"Grandson is a Dry Enforcer.
Grandpa is a Legger--
All for one and one for all--
I'll never die a beggar.
Bill brings booze from Montreal,
Grandpa lets him through--
Oh, life's been rosy for us folks
Since the red-light laws went blue."

2
Pretty Sadie, aged fourteen,
To a lamp-post clings serene.
"What's the matter?" some may ask.
On her hip she wears a flask

Labelled "Tonic for the Hair"--
"Hic," says Sadie, "we should care!"
  "Father is a corner druggist--
Why should I abstain?
Brother is a counterfeiter,
Printing labels plain.
I can buy grain alcohol
As all the neighbors do;
And if you treat me right I'll lend
My formula to you."


3

Sits the plumber, man of metal.
Joining gas-pipes to a kettle.
'Neath the bed his wife is lying
Rather silent--she is dying
From some gin her husband gave her.
He's too busy now to save her.


"Things," he sings, "are looking upward;
I am making stills.
Soon we'll cook the stuff by wholesale,
Running twenty 'mills.'
What we make and how we make it
Doesn't cut no ice.
Anything you sell in bottles
Brings the standard price."


4

In the gutter, quite besotted,
Lies the drunkard, sadly spotted.
People pass with unmoved faces--
Why remark such commonplaces?

Just another Volstead duckling,
Rolling in the gutter chuckling:

"Over seas of milk and water,
Angels' wings a-flappin',
Now we're purified and holy,
Things like me can't happen.
Liquor's gone and gone forever--
Even the word is lewd:
Otherwise there's somethin' makes me
Feel like I was stewed."

IV--*Finale--A Short Interview with the Human Stomach*

Last night as I lay on my pillow,
Last night when they'd put me to bed
I spoke to my dear little tummy
And wept at the words that I said:

"My sensitive, beautiful tummy
That once was so rosy and pure!
My dainty, fastidious tummy--
O what have you had to endure?

"You once were inclined to be fussy;
You turned at inferior rye;
You moped at a dubious vintage
And shrieked if the gin wasn't dry.

"But now you are covered with bunions
And spongy and morbid and blue;
You bite in the night like an adder--
O say, what has happened to you?"

Then my sullen and sinister tummy
Rose slowly and spoke to my brain;
"Say, boss, what's the stuff you've been drinking
That fills me with nothing but pain?

"Today you had 'cocktails' for luncheon--
They tasted like sulphured cologne.
They--were followed by poisonous highballs
That fell in my depths like a stone.

"I am dripping with bootlegger brandy,
I ooze with synthetical gin;
And the beer that you make in the kitchen--
Ah, dire are the wages of sin!

"The cursed saloon has departed,
And well we are rid of the plague;
But I'm weary of furniture polish
With the counterfeit label of Haig.

"Yea, gone is the old-fashioned brewery
And the gilded cafe is no more...."
Here my tummy jumped over the pillow
And fell in a fit on the floor,

# THE CENSORSHIP OF THOUGHT
## ROBERT KEABLE

I knew a man, about a year ago, who published a novel upon which the critics fell with such fury this side the water at least, that whether in the body or out of the body, such was ultimately his state of bewilderment, he could not tell, and if I am asked to discuss "Prohibitions, Inhibitions and Illegalities" it is natural that the incident should be foremost in my mind. True, it is becoming increasingly the fashion for a parson to preach a sermon without announcing text, but modern preaching, like brief bright brotherly breezy modern services, does not seem to cut much ice. Therefore we will hark back to the manner of our forefathers and take the incident for a text. It affords an admirable example of nonsenseorship.

As is always done in approved sermons (but humbly entreating your forbearance, which is less common) let us consider the context, let us review the circumstances of the case in point. Our author left the lonely heart of Africa for the theatre of war in France. He left a solitude, a freedom, a beauty, of which he had become enamoured, for that assemblage of all sorts of all nations, in a cockpit of din and fury, known as the Western Front. He expected this, that, and the other; mainly he found the other, that, and this. Being desirous of serving the God of things as they are, he pondered, he observed, and, his heart burning within him, he wrote. He had no opportunity of writing in France, so he wrote on his return, away up in the Drakensberg mountains, alone, with the clean veld wind blowing about him and the nearest town an hour's ride away, and that but three houses when he reached it. He had seen vivid things and it chanced he was able to write vividly. There were twenty chapters in his novel and he wrote them in twenty days.

The novel finished, the MS. of it was despatched to nine publishing firms in succession, who silently but swiftly refused it. It only went to the tenth at all because there is luck in a round number, and it found a home because it found a free man. On the eve of its appearance, it was hung up for a month because it was felt that whereas the booksellers might display a book containing a certain passage which referred to a woman's bosom, they would not do so if it contained a plural synonym. (I offer abject apologies for these dreadful details.) And when it finally appeared, the main portion of the English Press cried to heaven against it, and a smaller section clamoured for disciplinary action. For a hectic month the author, who had simply and plainly written of things as they were, honestly without conception that anyone existed who would doubt their truth or the obvious necessity for saying them, sat amazed before the storm.

Now that incident, unimportant to the world at large as it is, does afford an admirable example of that censorship which is about us at every turn. True, in this case, the official censor remained silent. Although prepared to read passages from Holy Scripture in the witness-box, and challenge a denial of the facts, the author was not called upon to do so. He had previously given slight hints of the truth about the racial situation in South Africa in another book and had had that volume censored out of existence, but perhaps because this present work merely touched on morals the official censor decided to give him rope with which to hang himself.

He was hung, of course, rightly and convincingly, hung by the neck till he was dead. Thus a clergyman who took the book from a circulating library because of its Scriptural title, and whose daughters wrapped it in **The Church Times** and read it over the week-end, declined to meet him at dinner. A bishop cut him in the street. Very rightly and properly too. The book honestly, simply, undisguisedly, told the truth. Since then America has been good enough to recognise it.

But this is at least the first consideration of British censorship today: it must suppress the truth about most of the important things in life. Take the allied case of the Unknown Warrior. We are told that he was a crusader, that he was glad to die in a noble cause, that his valour deserved the Victoria Cross and his religion Westminster Abbey. In short he was a saint. But, one protests (a bit bewildered because it sounds so good) that was not the man I knew. The man I knew lived next door and was a damned good chap. The man I knew chucked up his business and left his home and risked his life because everybody was doing it, because it seemed there was a real mess-up, because one had to.

Also, it was a change. Oddly enough, Adam goes out from a modern office or a modern factory in order to hoe up weeds in the sweat of his brow and in danger of his life with barely a regret for the Paradise he has to leave. Besides Eve went with him. God, there were Eves in France! Women who knew how to make a man forget, women who didn't count the cost, women who loved for love's sake. And for this and other causes, the Unknown Warrior was extraordinarily bored at having to die, except that he came not to care so much so long as he was sure he was only to be asked to die. As for his valour--Well, said he, it's no use grousing, and if it's a question of bayonets, it had better be mine in the other chap's stomach. Besides we English-speaking peoples don't shout about our valour. And as for religion--Well, if there's a God why doesn't He stop this bloody war, or, anyway, where the blazes is He?

There you are. It's abominable to write like that. Here it is in print; isn't it disgraceful? You see, it happens to be true. But if men said that, loud enough and enough of them, there would be no more wars. No more wars? There would be no more Downing Street either, and an American army would march, as like as not, on Washington. Disgraceful! It's so disgraceful that I am not sure, as I write, that this article will ever be printed.

Now since the War it is noticeable that the spirit of censorship has very visibly increased its activities among us. There is little doubt of that and there is little doubt of the reason for it. The War, by tearing down shams and by stripping men and women to the essentials, forced many to see things as they are. The old lies were no use in that hour, nor the old conventions and beliefs. Men learned to look beyond them, and they learned not to be afraid to look. Partly it was no use being afraid in the War and men got out of the habit, and partly, having looked, they saw something so much better ahead. Or again the trend of modern civilisation was so unarguably revealed in all the stark horror of its inhumanity that men saw suddenly that it was better to be brave and revolt and be killed than be cowardly and submit and live.

A great many of those who saw did not survive to tell the tale, but some did. There are more men and women about today who are not to be put off with humbugs than ever there were before. Such folk make up an element in Society which the censors know to be something more than dangerous. They are men who cannot easily be bribed for they have seen through the worth of the bribe, who cannot be intimidated because they no longer fear, and who cannot be cheated because they have seen true values. Hence your new censorship and its methods. Rebels must be drowned in a babble of words. They must be suppressed by the action of the unthinking masses rolled up upon them. They must be ground to powder lest they should turn the world upside down.

That, then, is the basis of censorship. Fear. You can do most things in England today except tell the truth, or, at any rate, except tell the truth in such a way that people will believe you. At the time of the French Revolution there was a broadsheet in circulation which showed on one side Louis XVI in his coronation robes. He was a fine figure of a man. His flowing wig descended majestically to his broad shoulders and his shapely leg, thrust forth, dominated a world. But on the reverse, a pimply shrunken figure emerged from the bath. Shortly after publication they had a revolution in France.

Now the War circulated such another broadsheet in the world. Here is the official side of it. Marriage is made in heaven. Politicians are earnest, devoted men. One's own country always fights for Right without Fear and without Reproach. Millionaires are nearly always philanthropists. Capitalism is a just, kindly, and reasonable basis for Society. The General Confession has become the national prayer of Englishmen. Modern Civilisation is thoroughly healthy and every day it gets better and better. It is so. It must be so. ***What's that?*** You have known a politician. . . . Your friend is married and. . . . Brother, it is impossible. You must not say so anyway: the whole fabric of Society will be shaken. You must not think so for a moment.

***You must not think so***. That is the creed of the new censorship. And very sensible, too. It is an odd thing that the Middle Ages of the Inquisition were so nonsensical, judged by our standards. Grand inquisitors cared remarkably little how a man thought provided he did not say what he thought too publicly. If he went to church once a year he might be a Jew for all their interference. If he signed the Thirty-nine Articles he might use a rosary in his own home. If Columbus thought the world was round, he was welcome to go and see, but if Galileo said that the Church was wrong for saying the world was flat, there was nothing for it but to shut him up in prison. It was all rather stupid, but it was interesting.

For above all things, the limits of censorship were well defined. Censorship was based on hypotheses. It was conceived that Almighty God had established St. Peter as a censor of public faith and morals, but it was not maintained that he was established as the censor of art and literature and life. There was thus originality in all these affairs. In a mediaeval town every house was different, in a mediaeval cathedral no two pillars were alike, and in the dress of a mediaeval crowd was captured the colours of the rainbow. With an odd result. Men laughed at the devil in the freedom of their souls. They tweaked his tail on carven misericords, and in the mystery play he was invariably cast for the clown.

Further, and in close accord with this, a pleasant feature of the old Inquisition was that it tried and burnt you for the good of your own soul, and despite all calumnies and mis-representations on the part of later writers, that remained to the end the main motive of the rack and of the stake. Personally I find it hard to suppose that some such consideration in any way lightened the last hours of the victim, but at least it enlightens our judgment of the inquisitor. Heresy was to him, quite honestly, a form of lunacy. Public opinion agreed with him. It was a species of moral and mental hydrophobia, and the mass of men no more desired to be converted to heresy than we desire to be bitten by mad dogs. In their simple souls they abhorred and feared the thing. They attended an auto-da-fé as an act of faith, piety, and rejoicing. They might have been a Paris crowd watching the last hours of such a social pest and terror as Landru, except that it probably occurred to few of the Parisian sightseers to pray for that murderer's soul.

But the modern Inquisition, the neo-censorship, is out, not to save my soul, but the souls of my contemporaries. It does not imagine that I am preaching a hideous thing from which all men will revolt; it imagines that I am offering them something which they will gladly and readily accept. It does not judge me and my sayings and doings from the standpoint of an accredited representative of society, but from the standpoint of a non-accredited governor of society. It silences me for fear that I may be followed, not lest I should be damned. It does not censor me for speaking or acting against an established order in which everyone believes, but for speaking or acting against an order in which practically everyone has ceased to believe. "Burn him," cried Torquemada; "he has spoken what no one thinks." "Bury him," cries your modern censor; "he has thought what no one speaks."

Thus, today, the point is that you may not think. All the energies of the censorship are bent towards the prohibition of thought. For one penny, every morning, even if you are an Englishman in Paris, a daily newspaper will tell you what to think and castigate you if you think otherwise. No, it is three halfpence in Paris. But that is the idea. That is the great conspiracy. Certain news-items are regaled to me, certain news-items are suppressed, in order that I may not think amiss. Certain books are refused me, certain plays must not be produced, certain fashions are taboo, certain things may not be done, lest, by any chance, I should form the habit of thinking, lest I should step out of the throng and be myself. Lest I should make a venture of personal opinion, and be right.

The odd thing is that the average man lends himself to the deception and even plays his part in the great game. Of course he is not altogether to blame. The psychology of the method is so truly conceived. It is dinned into him so repeatedly that things are so, that black is white and white is black, that if you see it in Bottomley's **John Bull** it is so, that he honestly comes to believe the bunkum. For he, too, fears at his heart. He is a conservative animal. Men used to burn a heretic because they believed in God; now they censor him out of existence because if they did not believe in the Northcliffe press they would have nothing whatever in which to believe. Men used to believe in the Ten Commandments; now they accept Prohibition because if they did not accept some authority they would have to govern themselves. Men used to believe the Bible; now they believe the daily papers because if they did not they would be compelled to lift up their eyes and look on life.

But Robert Louis Stevenson wrote the whole truth and nothing but the truth a while ago. "If you teach a man to keep his eyes upon what others think of him, unthinkingly to lead the life and hold the principles of the majority of his contemporaries you must discredit in his eyes the authoritative voice of his own soul. He may be a docile citizen; he will never be a man." And Bernard Shaw was not far out when, in the Introduction to **Man and Super-Man**, he pointed out what amiable honest gentlemen the free-booters who built the Rhine castles were compared with your modern millionaires, newspaper-owners, and political bosses. The robber-baron risked his neck. The robber-baron played a game. The robber-baron mostly warred on his own mates who were also playing the game. But the robber-baron of today would enslave the souls of men because he has forgotten how else to enjoy himself.

The net result then is that we are fast abandoning any attempt to think for ourselves. Not merely is any attempt at original thought or action cleverly stifled with pillows much as the princes were smothered in the Tower, but the censors of our freedom shout so loudly and supply us with mental goods so cheaply that in the end we have no real mental power of choice left. A million advertisements tell me that all decent people shave with Apple-Blossom soap, and with Apple-Blossom soap I shave. A score of papers tell me Germany is undertaxed and can pay Reparations, and I sit quiet while France occupies the Ruhr. Or vice-versa, as the case or another may be. Every child goes to school and every school is under Government control and every Government teaches that it is good for you to be governed and for the world that it should govern. A few years ago we were told that we had to be organised and schooled and managed because the nation was at war, but the thing is fast becoming a habit, and we have now to be managed and schooled and organised because the nation is at peace.

It is indeed just here that censorship has gone mad. It must have been horribly unpleasant to burn at the stake, but at least you had the satisfaction of knowing that the man who lit the faggots had some shadow of reason behind him. He had at least an hypothesis. He acted reasonably in its application. He believed something; he believed it with some horse-sense; and he acted as the saviour of Society. But today our censors have nothing behind them. No one supposes them to be more moral, more charitable, more instructed than other men; still less does anyone suppose them to be more inspired or dowered with divine right. They do not defend a faith for which they, too, would die; they merely bolster up a position because in so doing they find bread and butter. They do not object to innovators because what they innovate is bad; they object to innovators because they innovate. They do not object to us because they believe that we tell lies; they object because they know that we tell the truth.

This, then, is all very well, but what is the end to be? The theologians have always said that Almighty God left man free to sin because He did not want automatons. It is exactly here, however, that your modern censors improve on the Deity. They do want automatons. Only automatons will face liquid fire and poison gas. Only automatons will live in a jerry-built cottage in a modern town and pay heavily for the privilege. Only automatons will vote correctly at elections and keep the political business going and allow everything to run on smoothly for the next war. Only automatons will agree to the lengthening of skirts from the knee to the ankle. And only automatons will acquiesce in a system of morality which is not built on divine revelation or even on social necessity, but on exploded superstitions and sex domination and the conventions of the propertied classes.

Thus the devil is coming surely hut steadily into his own. We have already half-accepted an inverted order, allowing that all the good tunes are his and attributing to him things which he knows well enough he has no right to call his own. In a few years we shall neither use tobacco nor the grape, gifts of the good God, nor dance nor choose our own clothes nor laugh nor think. We shall scurry hither and thither before the flick of the devil's tail and be ready for the burning. We shall have sold our birthright of daring for an insipid mess of pottage: sold our right to choose and to spare, to slay and to leave alive, to be glad and to be sorry, to be martyrs if we would be, to explore, to risk, to win. We shall be docile and respectable, and the standard of our docility and respectability will have been set by men no better and no worse than we are. We shall be sober by act of Parliament, and moral--if it be morality--because we have lost the notion of being anything else. We shall be of no use whatever to God, and precious small beer for the devil.

And is there no way of escape? There truly is, Let any man ask the first censor that he sees by what authority he is censoring and who gave him that authority. Let him ask by what standards he is judging and in whose interests, and let him tell him what he thinks of his standards and interests. Let him say BOO and see how foolish the goose can look. Laugh, for Neo-Puritanism cannot stand laughter. Much else it can stand, but not that. Don't argue; the old enemy is mighty good at words. Don't hit; there are few of you strong enough. But laugh, laugh honestly, and go on laughing, for it is the only invincible weapon in the world. There is no more merry music either, and it is the melody for--Men.

## THE UNINHIBITED FLAPPER
## HELEN BULLITT LOWRY

Two generations ago the girl was "damned." One generation ago she was "ruined." Now, according to the best authorities and her own valuation, she has just played out of luck.

So that for the reformers and prohibitionists, the censors and the woman's club resolutionists! Their bi-product is Miss Twentieth Century Unlimited, the one uninhibited creature in a Volsteaded civilisation. Controls--of liquor and of birth--have given us The Flapper. The official reformers, reinforcing the sagging inhibitions and corsets of the nineteenth century, were just the final impetus needed to drive her out into the open.

The flapper is released from the strangle hold that is throttling the rest of us. If somebody makes a law for her, she promptly and blithely breaks it, the pocket flask for the moment being the outward and visible sign of the spirit--and spirits--of her wide-flung rebellion. It is the milepost between the time that was and the time that is, that flask, and to it we owe the single standard of drinking.

A half generation ago the sub-debs did not indulge in anything more relaxing than coca cola. And even first and second year debbies did their drinking from glasses issued by the hostess, not in triplicate. If a young man of the period imported a flask from the outside, that young man was promptly dropped from polite society, no matter how stringent was the shortage of dancing beaux. They called a flask a "bottle of whiskey" in those days.

Wild oats were reserved for the boys at college. If you were of Eve's sheltered sex, you really had to become a member of the Fast Young Married Crowd before you could get a look in. That Fast Young Married Crowd was the first to come out of the biological fastnesses of the Mid-Victorian era into the cocktails and jazz of our Mid-Victrolian period.

Moral: You had to keep yourself the kind of a girl you'd been told a man want-ed to marry, if you ever wanted to join in a cocktail party and slide down the ban-isters uninhibited--as rumor had it the Fast Young Married Crowd was doing on its orgies. Over the border of matrimony lay the mysteries of the gay wild life.

In that era before our morals were legislated, being "that kind of a girl" was a trying responsibility. There was an approved technique that every wise virgin had to master. It consisted of letting each man, on whom she conferred her favors, think that she really was in love with him. She called it "being engaged." And,--if per-chance she came to possess a harem of fiancés,--remember that the young things of the period were not so well able to conduct their own courtings as our present-day emancipated flappers. They still had to depend on what the tide washed in. They still did their picking from those that picked them--and sorted 'em over at their leisure.

Then, too, a half generation ago, we had not read our Freud. We did not know the jargon of sex. Both man and girl were apt to call "in love" the emotion which our present-day young things frankly call something else. Thus came it that the pet-ting parties of the period operated under the left wing of a near-engagement.

Yet there was a weakness to the system. Each fiance had the lordly impression that he "possessed" the lady of his choice. And the minute the male feels that he possesses a woman, he can get all the psychology of "riding away" and leaving her. Our Freudian flappers are better strategians. Man simply can't labor under the im-pression that he possesses a young person, if her lingo is calling the once sacred kiss just a "flash of pash." Applied slang is a great leveller of romance.

For times have changed since it was good form for a maid to avoid the crass mention of sex. With prohibition has come such an outburst of Get Moral Quick legislation that the reaction is now being felt throughout the length and breadth of the flapper. The legislators would lengthen the skirts to protect the defenceless male from a chance thought of legs and the like. Whereat the flapper retaliates by conversing pretty ceaselessly about--well, say associated subjects.

Last season the writer, being of the genus Successfully Single, woke up with a start to realize that two desirables had toyed with her hook--and retreated. One of them had even exited, uttering a fatal accusation about a "trammelled soul." Such a warning calls for a taking of stock. And this is what I found: Because of the flappers and the way they run shop, the whole technique of the man game has changed. My method, alas, had become as out of style as a pompadour Gibson hat. Where once girls pretended to know less and to have experienced less than they actually had, now they pretend to more. Therein lie all the law and the social profits. Therefore Rule One of these dauntless rebels reads: It is not an insult but a compliment for an admirer to explain that his intentions are frankly carnivorous.

To my ten-year-old technique had still been clinging the cobwebs of the past, when even Launcelot's intentions were painted as slightly honorable. But now--the shades of Alfred Lord Tennyson help us!--it has become the smart procedure to take Man's bold bad intentions right out into the conversation and pretend to be tempted by them.

The truth of the matter is that those pseudo-engagements of the fox-trot decade really were furnishing a charge account psychology. Man could close his eyes and whisper, "Some day, my own," and still go nicely on a ***Ladies' Home Journal*** cover design of "Under the Mistletoe." But, when our flapper is not even pretending to him that she is going to marry him, and when he is not even pretending to himself that he is going to marry her--well, the whole sex game has then been put on a frank cash and carry basis.

Mark well, however, these worldly-wise young things of this the third year of our Prohibition are not necessarily less virtuous technically than their own crinolined grandmothers. Only these days they are not bragging about their virtue.

"And have all the men afraid of you, for fear they'll be responsible for teaching you something," explains one practical miss. "Men like to find you in stock, ready-taught. We know how to take care of ourselves--so we let them think what they want." In short, the whole new game, as the earnest disciple from the half generation ago learned it, is not to reveal the dark secret that you abide by the Ten Commandments. Man must not suspect that you are unattainable. He must just think that he has not attained you--yet. If you want to compete with the flappers, you've got to play by the flapper rules. Check your conversational inhibitions!

And if by chance there be any inhibitions left over, Prohibition has obligingly introduced new opportunities for privacy, that will help you check them too. When a couple strays off now from group formation, there's a perfectly good alibi available of finding a sheltered spot for a drink. Where once it really wasn't good form to go to a man's hotel room, now it is the national custom for the owner of hootch to register a casket for his jewel--and then invite the young things in, one by one. A flapper these nights can retire to that hotel bedroom for an hour in the middle of a dance. The girl is not "talked about," and the place is not "pulled." Even the house detective knows that she is innocently drinking a drink.

Thus has this rebel young generation forced out into the open country with it all the contented young women in their late twenties and early thirties, who may not have been feeling rebellious at all. And the wives of forty-five also, to compete all over again for their own husbands. For "poaching" on the wifely preserves has become the favorite flapper sport!

"Married men," having been forbidden to unmarried young persons for three chaste generations, our flappers, bi-product of inhibition, are promptly appropriating the husbands. This one item of the flapper raid on the married men has done more than the entire twentieth century put together to change the smug structure of American society, and bring us back to normalcy.

Before 1865 no Southern belle considered herself worth her salt unless all the courtly old married men in the country kissed her hand and competed with the young blades for her quadrilles. But when black persons stopped buttoning up the shoes of the Quality, America entered upon her 1870's, her sombre brown stone fronts, and her cloistered husbands. The money for doing society had simply passed into the hands of the descendants of Miles Standish and Priscilla, who carried their consciences into their sober mansions with them. The Age of Innocence was upon us, and has clung close ever since.

From that fatal day on to 1917 each oncoming debutante was taught by her mother to give unto the genus, married man, her most impersonal manner, lest she provoke his "undesirable attentions." If poaching was done, it was from behind a tree. Unmarried girls knew that their place was not in somebody else's home in those days. The wives could protect their preserves by the simple expedient of "talking about" any unmarried young female caught on the married reservations.

And so it came to pass that the pick of the men were posted, because, as fast as a callow youth gets worth marrying, somebody promptly marries him. The Fast Young Married Crowd was a closed corporation and played exclusively within itself; the female of the species had to compete only with females of equal tonnage. The only sylph-like temptation that a husband could encounter was a dissolute person whose reputation had already been ruined--and she didn't count, because nobody invited her to parties anyway. A wife could get as fat as she wanted to in those days.

Even today that same leisurely life might exist for the wives. Even today the wives might be resting their feet under the bridge tables, secure in the consciousness that no bobbed haired young poacher was daring to dance with their husbands, if they had just let prohibitions enough alone--if they had only not been swept away by the high sport of gossiping about our Wild Young People, which struck the country in the summer of 1920. This gossip was an intrinsic phase of the virtue wave which always immediately precedes a crime wave.

The wives just at this point, instead of sitting tight, made the strategic mistake of turning the full force of the ammunition of gossip, which should have been saved for defending husbands from poachers, into an offensive attack on the flapper's lip stick, on her cigarettes, and on her petting parties. Whenever two or three wives were gathered together, their topic was our Wild Young People. That summer, too, saw the launching of that now seasoned romance about the checking of corsets. The resolutions at clubs were being resolved. The preachers were sermonizing. The upstate legislators were drafting bills against flappers' smoking cigarettes.

Human nature can be pushed just so far. Instead of reforming, the young things apparently decided one might as well lose a reputation for stealing a husband as for smoking a cigarette. The whole arsenal for combating poachers blew up.

To make matters worse, in the excitement of the virtue wave our Wild Young People had been attacked as a group instead of as individuals. That was the second mistake. The whole strength of gossip consists in selecting one member of the clan for calumny, to stand out disgraced and alone among her exemplary sisters. Because the flappers had been gossiped about *en masse*, the whole reason for not being gossiped about had ceased. The poacher of that half generation ago had been the kind of a girl who stalked her game alone.

But, when all the girls in town are seeking to steal your husband, what are you going to do about it, if you are a woman of forty-five with a heaviness around the hips and a disinclination to learn the camel walk? Nor can you get the poachers off the scent by crossing the trail with an eligible bachelor. Logically, the young things should have enough sense to ignore a preempted husband and attend to the serious business of getting themselves husbands. But they haven't. They seem to prefer the husbands of the other women. And curiously, the more they engage in this exotic sport of poaching, the less keen they become about owning a property for somebody else to poach on. The real interstate joke on Puritanism is that the flapper, who flaps because Puritanism has driven her to it, will automatically bring about its cure. The whole vitality of Puritanism rests on the unswerving principle of letting not thy right hand know what thy left hand doeth, if thy left hand is doing something it shouldn't. Puritanism could not last out a week-end without the able assistance of the standardized double life.

And that is just what the flappers refuse to respect. They are even insisting on being taken along on the parties, which, by all the rules of Rolf and Comstock should be confined to man's double life. Where the chorus lady was once the only brand that had the proper and improper equipment to jazz up an evening, now mankind has come to prefer the flapper, who drinks as much as the Broadwayite, is just as peppy and not quite so gold-diggish.

"It is so simple," smiles Barbara nonchalantly blowing her smoke rings. "You old dears set man an impossible standard. As he had always to be pretending holy emotions whenever he was around you he just naturally had to get away half the time, to rest the muscles of his inhibitions. Why, you funny old things actually drove man into his double life, just as you made all of his best stories have two editions, one for a nice girl and one for--well say one not so nice. Our crowd has done more than all of your silly old social hygiene commissions to bring nearer the single standard--by going part way to meet him."

The preachers are wasting their time when they rail that the flappers are painting their faces like "fallen women." Of course they are painting them that way--for the very good reason that mankind has demonstrated too unmistakably that that kind of woman has "a way with her."

Not so long ago cosmetics became a moral issue. The curl rag was the only beautifier that somehow never lost its odor of sanctity--and that was doubtless because curl rags were a perfectly logical part of the long-sleeved Canton flannel nightgown civilization. Curls couldn't be so very wrong when they were so frightfully unbecoming in the making. And so the "good woman" handed over intact to her weaker sister every beautifier that the world had been eight thousand years accumulating.

Slowly, timidly the allurements returned. The talcum powder bought for baby surreptitiously reached the nose. When the half generation ago was young, we had adopted a certain lip salve, just one shade darker than the way lips come, explaining, to save our reputations, that we were keeping our lips from chapping. Rouge too had come coyly, back--but--and here's the gist of the whole matter--in polite society paint was put on to imitate nature.

We were still doing our make-up as man conducted his double life--with intent to deceive the general public. We still belonged at heart to the Puritan era, in spite of our wicked fox-trot. All may have been artificial below the neck, from our Gossard corsets with their phalanx of garters on to our hobble skirts. But above the neck, we pretended it was natural.

The flapper has changed all that. She has turned the lady up side down, as well as the world. For the flapper is *au naturale* below the neck. Above the neck she is the most artificially and entertainingly painted creature that has graced society since Queen Elizabeth. With one bold stroke of a passionately red lip stick, she has painted out Elaine the Fair and the later-day noble Christie Girl and painted in an exotic young person, meet to compete alike with a Ziegfield show girl, with a heaven-born Egyptian princess or even a good Queen Bess, who could not move her face after it was dressed up for the morning. And Bess was the Virgin Queen. The American-Victorian is indeed the only era in history when cosmetics became a moral issue. Even in dour Cromwellian England, rouge registered the wrong politics but not immorality. We are merely getting back to normalcy in cosmetics--back behind the dun wall of the Victorian era.

And it is the flapper who has done it for us. What's more, she has done it frankly and purposefully--because the reformer, in his naive innocence, has explained to her that what she is doing is wicked and will get that kind of "results." Similarly those of 'em who had not yet taken off their corsets at dances, promptly did so when shocked elders began repeating the corset checking story. Dear heart, the only reason that they had not done so before was because the little dears hadn't heard that the worst people were using ribs instead of whalebone that season.

Vice would die out from disuse, if the reformers did not advertise.

# THE WOWZER IN THE SOUTH SEAS
## FREDERICK O'BRIEN

All over the South Seas the censor has had his day. From New Guinea to Easter Island, he has made his rules and enforced them. Often he wrote glowing pages of prose and poetry about his accomplishments, for reading in Europe and America. He was usually sincere, and determined. He felt that it was up to him to make over the native races to suit his own ideas of what pleased God and himself. When he had the lower hand, he prayed and strove in agony to change the wicked hearts of his flock to Clapham or Andover standards; he suffered the contumelies of heathen jibes, and now and again--often enough to make a cartoon popular--he was hotpotted or baked on hot stones as a "long pig." When he converted the king or chief, and he always directed his sacred ammunition at the upper classes, he took advantage of every inch of spiritual and governmental club put in his hand, and smote the pagan hip and thigh. His sole effort was to make the South Seas safe for theocracy, and to ***strafe*** Satan.

Of course, he was a missionary. It is doubtful if any other urge than a religious one could have infused into those canny migrants of the past century the extraordinary zeal that characterized their singular labors in the exquisite and benighted isles of the tropics.

To leave the melancholy and futuristic atmosphere of seminaries and bethels where the ghosts and penalties of millions of sins cast down their hearts, where few baths and drab clothes, dark homes and poor food, made all conscious of dwelling in a vale of tears, and after half a year or more of hard, ship fare and the rough discipline of a tossing windjammer, to find themselves in the most magnificent scenes on the globe, and amid the richest bounty, was trial enough of the unstable soul of man. That they--most of them--resisted the temptations of the tropical demon, that they continued to preach fire and brimstone, to remain flocked and shod, pantaletted and stayed, is proof enough of their cementation to the rock of ages.

The men were even subjected to direr spells. They were youths, the rude boys of farm and hamlet, schooled in simple studies, untried by the wiles of siren blandishments. If married, their courtships had been without passion, and their wedded years without competition, and generally without other incidents than children.

A typical union of this kind I find in an old diary of the wife of one of the most famous propagandists of the American God in Polynesia. He was of Yale and Andover, and she of Bradford, the daughter of a Marlboro deacon. She was twenty-four and he a little older when her cousin called upon her at her Marlboro home, to ask if she would "become connected with a missionary now an entire stranger, attach herself to a little band of pilgrims, and visit the distant land of Hawaii."

"What could I say? We thoroughly discussed the subject. Next week is the anticipated, dreaded interview of final decision. Last night I could neither eat nor close my eyes in sleep."

The suitor came. "The early hours of the evening were devoted to refreshments, to free family sociality, to singing, and to evening worship. Then one by one the family dispersed, leaving two of similar aspirations, introduced as strangers, to separate at midnight as interested friends.

"In the forenoon, the sun had risen high in the heavens, when it looked down upon two of the children of earth giving themselves wholly to their heavenly Father, receiving each other from his hand as his good gift, pledging themselves to each other as close companions in the race of life, consecrating themselves and their all to a life-work among the heathen."

After six months on the wave, she approaches the "land of darkness whither I am bound. When I reflect on the degradation and misery of the inhabitants, follow them into the eternal world, and forward to the great day of retribution, all my petty sufferings dwindle to a point."

They anchor, and "soon the islanders of both sexes came paddling out in their canoes, with their island fruit. The men wore girdles, and the women a slight piece of cloth wrapped around them, from the hips downward. To a civilized eye their covering seemed to be revoltingly scanty. But we learned that it was a full dress for daily occupation."

The note of nudity this really remarkable woman struck at her first sight of the welcoming savages, was the keynote of the new domination of the islands from Hawaii to Australia. The censors were convinced that it was a state of ungodliness. Their reasoning was based on the fig leaf tied about them by the first man and woman when they became conscious of sin, and it proceeded to the logical teaching that the less of the body exposed the more godly the condition. When they found this nakedness associated with a relation of the sexes utterly opposed to their own, and when, especially, the first white wives on the South Sea beaches, found the joyous, handsome, frolicsome women of the islands, making ardent love to their husbands, the innate heinousness of bodily bareness became fixed as a guiding star towards bringing the infidel to the true worship.

Clothe them and sanctify them, became the motto. From the wondrous Marquesas valleys to the American naval station of Samoa, the bonnet, the bonnet of a half century ago, is the requirement of decency in the coral or bamboo church, as it is in the temples of New York. The nightgown or Mother Hubbard of Connecticut became the proper female attire for natives in the house of God, and thus, by gradual establishment of a fashion, in their straw homes, and everywhere. Chiefesses were induced to don calico, and chiefs the woolen or denim trousers of refinement. The trader came to sell them, and so business followed the Bible. Tattooing, which, with the Polynesians and Melenesians, was probably a race memory of clothing in a less tropical clime, was condemned bitterly by the white censors as causing nudity. A man or woman whose legs and body were covered with marvellous arabesques and gaudy pictures of palms and fish was not apt to hide them under garments.

And here the censor also had an ally in the trader. The two joined, unwittingly, to break down both the old morale of the pagan and the new morality of the converts. The censorious cleric said that the Lord disliked nakedness, or, at least, that unclothedness was unvirtuous, while the seller of calico and alcohol advised the purchase of his goods for the sake of style. He ridiculed tattooing and nudity, but he also laughed with ribaldry at the religious arguments. The confused indigene, driven by admonition and shame put on the hot and griming stuffs, and finally, had them kept on him by statute. The censor in the South Seas achieved his highest reach of holy effort. He had made into law the *mores* his sect or tribe had coined into morals, and was able to punish by civil tribunal the evildoers who refused to abide by his conception of the divine wish.

But here, old Mother Nature revolted. All over the world it would appear that she is not in touch with the divinity that shapes the ends of the censors. The clothing donned by the natives of the South Seas killed them. They sweated and remained foul; they swam, and kept on their garments; they were rained on, and laid down in calico and wool, They abandoned the games and exercises which had made them the finest physical race in the world, and took up hymn books and tools. The physical plagues of the whites decimated them. They passed away as the tiaré Tahiti withers indoors. The censored returned to the rich earth which had bred them, and taught them its secrets and demands. Only a mournful remnant remains to observe the censorship.

But the curious spirit of inversion which tries to make the assumed infinite of a finite nature, which had sacrificed a race to an invented god, persists even in the South Seas. One of the most distinguished authors, who has chosen that delectable clime for his researches was arrested for napping on his own ***paepae*** partly clothed. The parson informed upon him, and the ***gendarme*** fined him. In the British South Seas, where I was recently, prohibition had cast a blight upon the more poetical whites. I remember one night when my vessel was anchored for a few hours in the roadstead of a lonely island, a group of civil servants and a minister of the Church of England had come aboard to buy what comforts they might from our civilized caravan. They sat on deck clinking glasses occasionally, talking of cities where a man might be freed from the "continuous spying of the uncoo good." That was the phrase they used, being English or Scots, and when the word was passed that we up-anchored with the turn of the tide at midnight, they sang in a last burst of lively furor a song of Dionysian regret. One stanza lingers with me:--

Whack the cymbal! Bang the drum!
Votaries of Bacchus!
Let the popping corks resound,
Pass the flowing goblet round!
May no mournful voice be found,
Though wowzers do attack us!

In the darkness I called to them as they went down the gangway into their boat, "What is a wowzer?"

"'E's a bloomin' ---- 'oo wants to do unto others wot 'e's bleedin' well done to 'imself."

The wowzers are more active in Hawaii, the most temperate portion of Polynesia, than in the Maori isles of New Zealand. A law passed at the last session of the Hawaiian legislature prohibits "any person over fourteen years of age from appearing upon the streets of Honolulu in a bathing suit unless covered suitably by an outer garment reaching at least to the knees." There is a ferment in Honolulu over the arrest and punishment of offenders against this new censorship. It is the result of the control by the spiritual, or perhaps, lineal, descendants of the first South Sea censors, of the great grand-children of those men who wore the girdles of leaves at the landing of the Marlboro school teacher a hundred years ago. The girdle-wearers are members of the Hawaiian legislature--soon to be succeeded by Japanese-native-born--and the censors, likely, are wives of financiers and sugar factors. Again the feeble remnant of the Hawaiian race voted against the girdle.

A friend of mine, grandson of the estimable missionary and his bride of the New England of a century ago, thus comments upon the law in a paper sent to me:--

The facts which caused the passage of the law were, that certain residents of Waikiki were donning their bathing suits at home, walking across and along the public streets to the sea and returning in the same state of undress.

If the bathing suits had been of the old-style no objection to this would have been made. The woman's bathing suit of the olden days were a cumbrous swaddling garment, high-necked, long-sleeved, full-skirted, bloomer-breeched and stockinged.

Simultaneously with the outbreak of the street parade era, above noted, there came with spontaneous-combustion-like rapidity, a radical change in the style of female bathing suits "on the street at Waikiki."

First the sleeves, then the stockings, then the skirts, then the main portion of the garment covering the legs, successively disappeared, until the low-necked, sleeveless, legless one-piece suit became "the thing"; and women clad in garments scantier than the scantiest on the ballet stage, were parading Kalakaua avenue in the vicinity of the Moana hotel, to the scandal and disgust of some; the devouring gaze of others; and the interested inspection of whomsoever chose to inspect!

It was a startling sight to the uninitiated--probably unduplicated in any other civilized country.

The South Pacific or the heart of Africa would probably have to be visited to find virtuous women so scantily clad, making such exhibition of their persons in public-more particularly on the public streets.

This scantiness of dress became the subject of protest, of justification, of discussion in press, in public and in private throughout the community.

The practice was violently attacked as tending to lewdness and scandal; as vigorously defended as a question of personal taste and liberty, and as a matter concerning safety and comfort in swimming.

Those "old-style suits" he refers to, "full-skirted, bloomer-breeched" were the godly ones brought to Hawaii by the censors, but which gradually disappeared with the influx of rich tourists from America, and the importation by Honolulu merchants of the flimsier and less concealing kind. This new generation of whites that has sought escape from the "cumbrous, swaddling garment" embraces the flapper, who at Waikiki is a beautiful and wholesome sight. Browned by years of exposure to the beach sun, charmingly modelled, and with the grace and freedom of limb of the surf-board rider and canoeist, she has no consciousness of guilt in her emergence dripping from the sea, in her lying in the breeze upon the sand, nor in her walks to and from her bungalow nearby. And she refuses to be censored.

The commentator, proprietor of the oldest newspaper in the islands, and himself a noted diplomat, lawyer and revolutionist--he took up a rifle against Liliuokalani--says so:--

The law has been observed by a few, ignored by a few, and caricatured by the many. It is not an uncommon thing to see a woman walking the streets in Waikiki in the scantiest of bathing suits, with drapery of the flimsiest suspended from her shoulders and floating behind upon the breeze.

The police have made a few feeble and spasmodic attempts to persuade observance of the law, with some ill-advised attempts to enforce individual ideas of propriety on the beach itself.

On the whole, the law is either openly and flagrantly violated or rendered farcical by the contemptuous manner of its semi-observance.

And, cautiously but firmly, the grandson of the first missionaries to Hawaii, himself living six decades in Honolulu, a church member and supporter of all evangelical and commercial progress, gives advice to the people of his territory. Urging that those opposed to the bathing suit law try legally to secure its repeal, but that all obey it while it is on the statute books, he says:--

As to the question of attire on the beach, there are modest and immodest women to be found everywhere, regardless of their clothes. It is impossible to legislate modesty into a person who is innately immodest, and it is therefore useless to try and do so. The attire of a woman on the beach at Waikiki as well as her conduct elsewhere, should therefore be left to the individual woman herself.

That is the last word of a very shrewd, wealthy, experienced, religious son of censors. But wowzerism dies hard in America or in the South Seas. The Anglo-Saxon American has it in his blood as an inheritance from the rise of Puritanism four hundred years ago, while with many it is an idiosyncrasy to be explained by the glands regulating personality. In fact, I feel that this is the enemy the would-be free must fight. We must attack and extirpate the wowzerary gland.

# REFORMERS: A HYMN OF HATE
## DOROTHY PARKER

I hate Reformers;
They raise my blood pressure.

There are the Prohibitionists;
The Fathers of Bootlegging.
They made us what we are to-day--
I hope they're satisfied.
They can prove that the Johnstown flood,
And the blizzard of 1888,
And the destruction of Pompeii
Were all due to alcohol.
They have it figured out
That anyone who would give a gin daisy a friendly look
Is just wasting time out of jail,
And anyone who would stay under the same roof
With a bottle of Scotch
Is right in line for a cozy seat in the electric chair.
They fixed things all up pretty for us;
Now that they have dried up the country,
You can hardly get a drink unless you go in and order one.
They are in a nasty state over this light wines and beer idea;
They say that lips that touch liquor
Shall never touch wine.

They swear that the Eighteenth Amendment
Shall be improved upon

Over their dead bodies--
Fair enough!
Then there are the Suppressors of Vice;
The Boys Who Made the Name of Cabell a Household Word.
Their aim is to keep art and letters in their place;
If they see a book
Which does not come right out and say
That the doctor brings babies in his little black bag,
Or find a painting of a young lady
Showing her without her rubbers,
They call out the militia.
They have a mean eye for dirt;
They can find it
In a copy of "What Katy Did at School,"
Or a snapshot of Aunt Bessie in bathing at Sandy Creek,
Or a picture postcard of Moonlight in Bryant Park.
They are always running around suppressing things,
Beginning with their desires.
They get a lot of excitement out of life,--
They are constantly discovering
The New Rabelais
Or the Twentieth Century Hogarth.
Their leader is regarded
As the representative of Comstock here on earth.
How does that song of Tosti's go?--
"Good-bye, Sumner, good-bye, good-bye."

There are the Movie Censors,
The motion picture is still in its infancy,--
They are the boys who keep it there.

If the film shows a party of clubmen tossing off ginger ale,
Or a young bride dreaming over tiny garments,
Or Douglas Fairbanks kissing Mary Pickford's hand,
They cut out the scene
And burn it in the public square.
They fix up all the historical events
So that their own mothers wouldn't know them.
They make Du Barry Mrs. Louis Fifteenth,
And show that Anthony and Cleopatra were like brother and sister,
And announce Salome's engagement to John the Baptist,
So that the audiences won't go and get ideas in their heads.
They insist that Sherlock Holmes is made to say,
"Quick, Watson, the crochet needle!"
And the state pays them for it.
They say they are going to take the sin out of cinema
If they perish in the attempt,--
I wish to God they would!

And then there are the All-American Crabs;
The Brave Little Band that is Against Everything.
They have got up the idea
That things are not what they were when Grandma was a girl.
They say that they don't know what we're coming to,
As if they had just written the line.
They are always running a temperature
Over the modern dances,
Or the new skirts,
Or the goings-on of the younger set.
They can barely hold themselves in
When they think of the menace of the drama;
They seem to be going ahead under the idea
That everything but the Passion Play
Was written by Avery Hopwood.

They will never feel really themselves
Until every theatre in the country is razed.
They are forever signing petitions
Urging that cigarette-smokers should be deported,
And that all places of amusement should be closed on Sunday
And kept closed all week.
They take everything personally;
They go about shaking their heads,
And sighing, "It's all wrong, it's all wrong,"--
They said it.

I hate Reformers;
They raise my blood pressure.

# PROHIBITION
# FRANK SWINNERTON

I shall never forget the shock I received when an American woman, newly arrived in England, gave me her impressions of London. She was distinctly pleased with the town, and when I rather foolishly asked if she had been terrified by our celebrated policemen, she said, "Why, no. I was in a taxicab yesterday, and the driver went right on past the policeman's hand, stealing round where he'd no business to go. And the policeman just said, 'Here, where you going? D'you want the whole of England?' Why, in New York, if he'd done that, he'd have been in prison inside of five minutes!"

I wonder if it will be understood how terrible disillusion on such a scale can be. I had been thinking of the United States for so long as the home of the free and the easy that it was hard to bring myself to the belief that the police there were both peremptory and severe. I had thought them all Irishmen of the humorous, or "darlint" type. It seems I was mistaken. The little--I am now afraid misleading-- paragraphs which from time to time appear in the English papers, saying that there has been a hold-up on Fifth Avenue, or that the Chief of Police in some great city has been found to be the head of a gang of international assassins, that things called Tammany and graft and saloons flourish there without let or hindrance, had attracted me to the United States. I wanted to live in such a country. Here, I said, is a place where every man's hand is for himself, where the revolver plays its true part, and where, with the aid of a humorous Irish policeman, who will find me stunned by a sandbag and take me to his little home in 244th Street and reveal the fact that he is descended from Cuchulain, I can be happy.

At first I thought that my friend must be exaggerating. Not lightly was I prepared to let my dream go. But I am afraid that my confidence in America as the home of freedom needs a tonic. She may have been right, although it seems unbelievable. When I thought the problem out clearly I came to the conclusion that there was a sinister sound about that comment upon our policemen. Were they losing control of us? Apparently not. I had trouble on the road with a policeman over the rear light of my car. There is no doubt that England is efficiently policed. And so my mind stole back to America with a new uneasiness. I recollected tales which I had heard about sumptuary laws regulating the dress of American women, both in and out of the water. I saw the police invading restaurants and snatching cigarettes from the mouths of women. I saw drink being driven underground by Prohibition. I began to question whether I should really like to live in the United States after all. I asked those of my friends who had been to America.

They told me that if I visited America I should be regaled privately with champagne from the huge reserves of private wine-cellars, but that as a resident I should be forbidden to drink anything that enlivened me. It was a great shock. I am not yet recovered from it. I see that I shall after all have to live quietly in England with my pipe and my abstemious bottle of beer. And yet I should like to visit America, for it has suddenly become in my imagining an enormous country of "Don't!" and I want to know what it is like to have "Don't" said by somebody who is not a woman.

I have always hated the word "Don't." I hated it as a child, and I hate it still. It is a nasty word, a chilling word, associated with feelings of resentment, of discipline, of prohibition. Yes, that is it, of course, Prohibition. I find that it is Prohibition which makes my throat so dry. I thought it was a human characteristic, when anybody said, "You're not to do that!" to do it at once in case there should be any misunderstanding. I should be frightened to say "Don't!" to anybody, because I feel sure it would precipitate unpleasantness. Is America so different from the rest of the world that it likes having "Don't!" said to it? I cannot think that. What occurs to me is that America has not yet worked out of its system the strain that the English Puritan fathers brought with them. It is a melancholy thought to me that it is really ancient English repression that is responsible for the present state of affairs. I feel very guilty, particularly as I have seen an article about myself in an English newspaper headed "A Modern Puritan." It is really I, and people like me, who have caused the great drink restrictions in the United States. I bow my head.

The truth is, I suppose, that people in the United States take life more seriously than we do in England. If you read any of the books which have been written in this country during the ages to show what sort of community is the ideal--I refer to such works as "Utopia" and "News from Nowhere"--there is never any differ-ence between them on one point. All the dwellers in these ideal states appear to be thoroughly idle. They have practically no work to do at all. All their time is spent in talk and sylvan wandering, with music and dancing round maypoles. There is no mistaking the fact that the Englishman's idea of life is confirmed and justifiable laziness. He wants what he calls leisure. Charles Lamb, a typically English author, wrote a poem beginning "Who first invented work?" He came to the conclusion that it must have been the Devil. The inference is clear. Observation confirms my view. It is not to be doubted that the average Englishman spends his life in schem-ing to make somebody else do the work that lies nearest to his hand.

Americans must be different. I believe they really like work. And I will give the Prohibitionists this handsome admission. I also work much better without stimulants. I mean, much harder. But on the other hand, I am less happy. Does an American feel happy in his work? Does the act of work give him a satisfaction which is not felt by an Englishman? I think that must be the explanation. But on the other hand there is this question of Puritanism. We tried it in England, and we had a severe reaction to libertinism. We maintain Puritanism only in our suburban districts, where there is exceedingly close scrutiny of all matters pertaining to con-duct; and in our theatres. In the suburbs it does not much matter, although it rather cramps our suburban style; but in the theatre it drives some of us to distraction. I will explain why.

Supposing a man wants to write a play, he at once thinks of getting it produced. An unproduced play is like an unpublished novel: practically speaking it does not exist. The author can read it, of course, and his wife can assure him that it is a great deal better than anything she has seen or read for years; but the author and his wife are both haunted by the fact that there is a masterpiece which is lying--not fallow, but unused and sterile. They grow dissatisfied. The savour of life is lost for them. They develop persecution mania, grow very conceited, and finally come to believe that only they of all the men and women alive truly grasp the essentials of life. They say, if this were the silly muck that most authors write, it would be produced, and then we should have our car and our servants and diamonds and titles and all the paraphernalia of happiness. As it is, we are doomed to silence and poverty, simply because George is too much of an artist to lower himself by writing what the public wants, and what the censor will pass. For I have not been outlining the diseased state of mind of the merely incompetent man who writes something that nobody will look at. I have been giving details of one of those men who have a moral message, and who desire greatly to spread it by means of the stage. He has written, let us say, a play in which the name of God appears, or a play wherein a young woman has a baby and does not wish to have a husband. The censor says that there must be no mention of God in plays performed on the public stage, and that young women who have babies must either have husbands or come to early graves of their own seeking. Very well, what happens? I have described the state of mind of a husband and wife who have a pet child--a play--which is lying heavy on their minds and hearts and hands. They are ripe for any temptation of the devil. And it comes. It always comes.

The devil dresses himself up in the guise of a Sunday play-producing society. The play is surreptitiously performed in a theatre to which admission can be obtained only by members banded together for just such emergencies. It is very badly acted by actors and actresses who have not been able to spare sufficient time from their daily work to learn their parts as well as they should have done. The audience comes full of a smug self-satisfaction at the thought that it is excessively intellectual and select, and that it alone can appreciate blasphemy or the vagaries of neurotic young women. It sits intellectually in the theatre, and watches the play. The author sits intellectually in his box, and intellectually accepts the plaudits of the audience. He lives thereafter in a highly intellectual atmosphere. He is driven to become a member of the secret play-producing society, and to watch other plays of a character not suited to the requirements of the censorship. He is morally a ruined man. He will never any more be a decent member of society, for he has become an intellectual. He has been taught to despise ordinary human beings, for they do not want to be wicked or silly, except in the normal humdrum way, and they have not seen his play and are not members of his play-producing society. He discovers that the censored is the only good art. He is driven to the reading of all sorts of Continental drama. He is made into an anti-English propagandist. He is like the person in the song, who,

"Praises every century but this, and every country but his own."

He has been lost for human kind, and is wedded to intellectualism and a sense of superiority to others for the rest of his miserable life. He institutes a new system of censorship of his own. It takes the form of sneering at and condemning anything that does not conform to his own ideas. He sniffs at all sorts of innocently happy people who are inoffensively pursuing their noisy course through life. He begins to hate noise. He makes a virtue of his abstention from ordinary pleasures. He speaks condescendingly of the "hoi polloi." As I said, he is ruined. He is no longer a man that one can talk to with any comfort, for his sense of superiority is intolerable.

To me there is nothing more terrible than the sense of superiority to others. It arises, not from merit or the consciousness of merit, but from sheer tin-like flimsiness of character. It arises from limited sympathies. The really great man, and the really sagacious man, is one to whom nothing is contemptible. To him, even the follies of his fellow-passengers are manifestations of human nature, revelations of the material from which scholars and politicians no less than drunkards and inconstants are gradually in course of time developed. Somebody described "conceit" to me the other day as egotism in which contempt for others is involved. It was agreed between us that egotism was normal, since happiness is not to be attained without a sense of personal utility to the world, and no objection was urged against it. Vanity was to be tolerated, because it was definitely social--a recognition of the existence and value of the good opinion of others; but never sense of superiority. And the sense of rebellion should be added to this other sense, as equally to be regretted. A young woman whose incredible acts of folly had spoiled half-a-dozen lives, including her own, recently encountered a young man whom she had jilted on the eve of her marriage to another, whom she had also left. The young man, still smarting under his ill-treatment, reproached her. He said, "What you want, my dear, is discipline." "Pooh!" she answered. "I'm *above* discipline!" The poor young man retired, unequal to the conversation. But the young woman went on her way, defiant and self-infatuated, believing that she really was superior to the opinions of others, the common decencies of conduct, the inevitable give and take of ordinary life. Driven to folly by lack of balance, she was learning to justify her folly by the argument for rebellion. Whether she will ever learn to control her actions I do not know, but rebelliousness from a fueling that one is too good to be governed by normal standards is not only arrogant and unsocial. It is silly. It is, to my mind, a criminal form of silliness. But it is one very widely accepted by the young and the unimaginative. It must therefore be recognized and combated.

It springs, perhaps, from disordered shame, which makes children noisily act in defiance of authority, particularly if there are others present to overhear. No children are worse-behaved than those who are over-controlled. The word "don't" at the breakfast-table produces more acts of violent rebellion than any amount of parental weakness. Unimaginativeness begets unimaginativeness. Rigidity in one person creates a counter-rigidity in the other. There is a thwarting upon both sides, a mutual shackle upon sweetness and understanding. A wildness of action arises, with loss of affection, respect, self-respect. And the vicious part of it is that children (we are all children, for we never grew up in human relations), once they are embarked upon an evil course, are driven by vanity to continue upon that course until they are exhausted, going from defiance to defiance; and ultimately building up a whole sophisticated gospel of axioms whereby rebellion is given warrant and virtue. The gospel of rebellion we know to be specious and without justification; but it is essential to us, as human beings, to maintain self-approval for our acts. If we cannot do this socially, by comparative standards, we do it unsocially, by subversion of those standards. Rebels are only prigs turned upside down or inside out.

The great defect of prohibition is that when it can be enforced by law it makes rebels who think there is something inconceivably clever in doing secretly that which the law forbids. They learn to think there is some subtle merit in evading the law. They encourage others to break the law, and so develop cliques and finally new and silly conventions. Or, prohibition has another effect. It makes a whole class who accept its rulings, and gradually these people, owing to a peculiarity which all gregarious animals seem to have, begin to believe that unless all are of their persuasion and of their number the fault lies with the rebels. First of all they consider themselves superior to the rebels, and despise them. Then, when they find that the rebels think that *they* are the superior class, in defying the law or the convention, a new set of notions arises, and this set of notions leads to persecution and to war. You cannot introduce any restrictive or prohibitive measure without developing fanatical conceit, narrow-mindedness, and intolerance, both in those who welcome the measure and in those who seek to ignore and even to defy its rulings.

The Puritanical attitude is almost wholly repressive, and naturally invokes force to aid its repressive measures. It did so in England centuries ago in the matter of the theatre, and we are living among all the rotten plays which have been written since, and the theatre is for the most part a place of ignominious diversion. The play-producing societies have nothing to produce that is worth producing, because the atmosphere which causes such plays as are written to be produced privately is not the healthy atmosphere from which masterpieces arise. It is an atmosphere impregnated with priggishness and a sense of superiority. It is an atmosphere, if there can be such a thing, of sterility. The same thing happens in other matters, and I do not feel at all certain that it may not happen with drink. If you say men are not to drink you create two new classes. There is of course the existing class that does not care for drink and is afraid of its effects to the point of wishing to keep it away from those who do like drink. That class already flourishes in most communities, and so I do not place it among any two classes which are created by the prohibition. The two classes are as follows-the class that submits, and gradually develops priggishness and self-satisfaction at being in the majority, and the class that rebels, and gradually develops priggishness and self-satisfaction at being in the minority. Both classes are objectionable, and I do not know which is the worse. They are both inevitable in a world of prohibitions, and if the United States, to which we are all looking as the real hope for intelligent civilization, is going to take away our beer and turn us into supporters of play-producing societies I cannot think what will happen to the world. Better a wicked world than a virtuous one. Better a world in which we can hope that there are people worse than ourselves than a world where we know that there cannot be any better.

## A GUESS AT UNWRITTEN HISTORY
## H. M. TOMLINSON

That fairly violent scuffling during the years 1914-1918, the opening skirmishes of the war between Organization and Liberty which our fore-fathers named so strangely the "War to End War," did not appear to conclude satisfactorily for the victorious nations, especially England. Actually it was an excellent ground for the founding of that Perfect State which, in the centuries that followed, arose on the lines laid largely by chance and the exigencies of that early scramble. Yet it is possible the victorious statesmen may not have guessed that they had done really well. The name by which the war of those remote years was popularly known is enough to show that the difficulties faced by those men at the end of the war may have obscured the good they had done. That name is itself clear evidence of the not unpleasing credulity and ridiculous but innocent desire of the people of that time.

After all, those peoples were not so long out of the Neolithic Age. Their memory was still strong of the freedom of their earlier wanderings when they could go where they liked, work at what suited them, eat and drink what pleased them, choose who should be their chief, and worship in any Temple which promised most personal benefits. It was, then, natural for them to make so amusing a mistake in the naming of their "Great War." They not only certainly imagined they were ending War, but they imagined, too, they had a right to end it, thinking that not only War, but every other act of the State, was for their decision. Their Governors, therefore, judged it wise to allow them this illusion to play with, so to distract their attention from the reality, which they would have resented. This illusion was known as Popular Government.

We may laugh at it now, but in those days the directing minds of great nations found that common illusion no laughing matter. Some who laughed at it openly discovered they had laughed on the wrong side of the guillotine. It is usual in this era of science, when control by the Holy State of the national mass-power, both of body and mind, is complete, and when national emotion is raised by Press and Pulpit whenever it is required and put wherever it is wanted, to ridicule the laxity of the statesmen who directed the nations in that early war. A little reflection, however, shows us that that laxity is but apparent. Those statesmen went as far as they dared, and dared a little more with each success they won. They discovered that control may be gained by announcing control to be necessary for some quite innocent object, and then using and retaining the power thus acquired for a real but undivulged purpose. Sheep, we are aware, never understand they are securely folded till the completing hurdle of the circuit is in its place, and then they soon forget it, and begin grazing; for all sheep want is grass, and perhaps a turnip or two to give content in a limited pasture.

It would be wrong for us, nevertheless, to blame those early folk for not understanding, as finely as we do, the true science of government to be complete and unquestioned mastery. We have learned much since then. Let us look back to those days for a moment, to get the just perspective. One of the first significant things we notice is that those people were free to criticize their politicians--baaing across the hurdles, as it were. That was why they had to have explained to them the "Objects of the War." They actually did not want to die. They were reluctant to go to battle unless they knew why they were going. True, it was easy enough to find a reason to satisfy them, but it is necessary for us to remember that they would not submit to mutilation and death without some reason. Much as their governors may have desired it, those primitives would not agree willingly to the total surrender of conscience, individual liberty, and of life, to "politicians," as the High Priests of the Holy State were then familiarly named. Individual conscience, therefore, had to be cajoled, had to be bamboozled, had to be hypnotized; and a man's liberty could not be taken from him unless he was helpless, or was looking, under clever political finger-pointing, the other way.

It was this almost intractable matter of personal conscience and liberty which was the cause of the angry disappointment following the Versailles Treaty which, illustrating still further the need for subtle tact in dealing with our hairy forefathers, was called a Peace Treaty.

What a light is thrown upon those distant days and peoples when that ancient document, the fragmentary relic of which is now treasured in the museum at Tobolsk, is examined with even the little knowledge we possess of the events immediately following it! For a time, we must believe, humanity then was deliriously bereft. One could almost believe the moon had a greater pull in those years.

"No more secret diplomacy!" historians tell us was one of the cries of the soldiers as they went to battle. There is considerable ground, too, for accepting the amusing traditional tale that even at the end of the war the then President of the American Republic (mainly confined at the time to the Western Continent), declared the first point for the guidance of the Peace Conference must be an open discussion of the covenant. And the first thing to happen when the war ended was the closing of the door of the council room by the peacemakers, who, naturally, were the very men with no other interest till that moment but the full pursuit of war; yet nobody noticed the door was shut, though nobody could hear what was going on inside the room. The faith in their politicians held by the natives of the backyard communities into which Europe was then divided--on the very eve, we see now, of the full continental control of international man-power by consolidated finance--was the measure of their annoyance when, too late, naturally, the fact that the old shackles from which they had been promised freedom were noticed to be riveted upon them several links tighter.

But it is not their faith, so happily youthful, which so reveals their ingenious minds as their resultant annoyance. That resentment illuminates the essential fact for us in studying their mentality as social animals. They really did accept without question, with open and receptive mouths and eyes shut, what was considered pleasing enough to fortify them in the trials of warfare. They were, difficult though it is for us to understand it, too vacant and generous to realize that the "Objects of the War" were but figments nicely calculated to get them busy. The figments--we must give credit to the leaders of the time-were indeed not un-imaginatively conjured up. Those inducing visions worked. They were accepted readily, and even with delight. It was sincerely believed that the pleasing dreams were substantial, that those chromatic vapours evoked by gifted statesmen were veritable promises of divine favor for meritorious endurance.

From that we can the more easily go with understanding to a study of the consequences of that attractive faith of undisciplined peoples so difficult to grasp for modern students, who witness daily the admirable submission of our own uniform herds to the divine ordinances of the High Priests of the Sacred Entity the State. Why, we even learn that the survivors of the not inconsiderable armies returned from the battlefields of 1918 with the innocent conviction that the gentlemen of England would keep a bond as faithfully as common soldiers! The hardest tasks of the statesmen of those days arose out of such extraordinary expectations, out of the ruinous supposition of the childish-minded that the honoring of a bond, the fulfilment of a promise in return for benefits received, is equally incumbent on everybody!

With that knowledge we begin to realise the difficulties of their statesmen. A careful computation shows us that in England, where indeed the lavish promises had been most picturesque, and where the tough idea of personal liberty took longest to kill, it required just four years of severe disciplinary measures and dry bread to reduce the masses generally to a pale, obedient, and constructive spirit. At first they would not work unless they wanted to, and then only at their own price. They pointed, when answering their masters, to the fact that the best-fed people never worked at all, and lived in the best houses. They refused to cancel the official contracts made with them, even when ordered to do so by the police. They behaved indeed, those ex-soldiers, as though it had been *their* war. Such a state of mind we in these days really find impossible to elucidate. It is rather like trying to read the spots on a giraffe. It is as inscrutable as the once general opinion that the community has a right to decide upon its own affairs.

Today we have reached that point in the evolution of society when uniformity is known to be more desirable, because more comfortable than liberty; and uniformity is impossible without compulsion. A man with a free and contentious mind is a danger to the community, for he destroys its ease. He compels his fellows to active thought, if only to refute him. This is a dissipation of energy, and a local weakening of the structure of the State. It is historically true that a few men with ranging and questioning minds have sometimes injected so strong an original virus of thought that the community has been changed in form and nature.

It was the mistake of the earlier nations to give little attention to these troublesome and subversive fellows, who always thought more of the truth than they did even of the inviolability of the High Priests of the State. They preferred to die rather than surrender the out-dated rights of man. Therefore they had to die. The rights of man cannot be allowed to stand in the way of a nation's perfect uniformity. It was many centuries before man realized that the only freedom worth having is freedom from the necessity for individual thought. Perfectly unembarrassed freedom, freedom in which the mind may be empty and sunny, and assured happily of not the slightest interruption from any unsanctioned unofficial idea, became possible to a community only after the sanitary measures were devised which sufficed against unexpected epidemics of speculative thinking.

This, we are sadly aware, took time; for the brightly-colored hopes sent skyward so long ago as 1914, and the vistas discovered as a consequence by young men whose eyes till then had been resting safely on the ground, and the daring and lively questioning that was aroused by the incessant nudging of sleeping minds, coincided, as it unluckily happened, with the beginnings when the "Great War" ended, of mass-production and international finance, so developing problems of government, the solving of which could not be reconciled with any admission of individual liberty and personal right. It was, therefore, the elimination of the notion of justice and liberty from common opinion which occupied statesmen from 1918 onwards.

Gradually the true social morality has been evolved--that one citizen should be so like all other citizens that his only distinguishing characteristic is his number; that the right ideal of citizenship, plain for all to follow, and ensuring the stability of society, is to be so loyal to the Holy State that an expression of a man's views in a gathering of his fellows will rouse no more curiosity than a glass of water. Obviously so desirable a similarity of mind and character, making disputation impossible, and preventing all dislike of the ordinances of the Sacred Entity, or Cabal of Inviolable Dispensers, a uniformity in which war and peace become merely the national output of a vast machine controlled by the Central Will, has been developed only through ages of Press Suggestion, popular education with a bias that was designed but was scarcely noticeable, the seizing and retaining of opportunities by legislators whenever public opinion was sufficiently diverted, and a development of chemical science and aeronautics which has been encouraged by the enlightened directors of the major industries.

The war which began in 1914 showed quite clearly, for example, the value of the Censorship. The instituting of this office was never questioned, for it was based on man's first impulse of obedience to superiors when faced by a sudden danger, caused by his fear of the unknown. More than that, the English were in a lucky state of exaltation at the time, and were ready to sacrifice everything to save from destruction what they were told was the ancient, exquisite, and priceless civilization of France. They did save it; but in the prolonged and costly process they learned more than they had known before of that civilization, as well as of their own; and so much of their fear of losing either was evaporated. By that time, anyhow, criticism was useless, because the Censorship then was empowered to deal even with a derisive cough when Authority was solemnly giving orders. Once the office of the Censor was set in its place unnoticed in a time of public nervousness and excitement, the rest was easy, for it became possible to bring all criticism within a law which was elastic enough to be extended even to those figments which merely worked on the timidity of unbalanced minds.

It became unpatriotic to express a dislike for margarine, when butter was prohibited. It was unpatriotic for a blind hunchback with heart disease to protest that he was no soldier, if he were ordered to the Front. For though the Censor, in the early period of that war, dealt merely with news and opinions which might aid the enemy, yet, as the value of adding to a nation's enemies became apparent to Authority, it became necessary to turn into enemies of the State those who denounced profiteers for turning blood into money, those who denounced generals for wasting the lives of boys in purposeless actions, those who spoke against the spending of the nation's resources to succor needy contractors, and those who asked whether the war was to go on till all were dead, or whether it might be stopped profitably at any time by using a little common sense. Luckily for the welfare of the community, this need for recognizing as enemies all, at home and abroad, who differed from the decision of the Central Will, a need which was the natural flower of that confidence which Authority acquired through discovering the ease of control, put within the power of the Censor by the time of the Peace Conference every possible form of protest, every call for light, every cry of pain, every demand that such a "horrible nonsense" as war should cease from human affairs, every plea for compassion and generosity.

Thus the problem of perfect government was engendered and simplified. It was at last possible to ensure, at least outwardly, a semblance of uniformity. The rest was a matter of evolution, till today only a particular enquiry will determine a man from a woman, though it may fail to determine a fool from a man. All are alike, all agree with what is officially announced by the Sacred Entity, and the nation is as loyal and homogeneous, as contented, as stable and industrious, as a reef of actino-zoal plasm. Thus the Perfect State has been built like a rock. The City of God has at last arisen; and in each of the uniform homes of its neuters, or workers, there is to be found the Patriotic Symbol--a portrait of a Sheep, enjoined by law to hang in a principal place, and bearing the legend "God Bless this Loyal Face."

Here, however, we see at once that such a right condition of the public mind could never have been acquired by a Censorship, by a mere prohibition, that is, of individual thinking and acting. That ensures merely a simulacrum of homogeneity. The appearance of general acquiescence may exist, though not the real thing. It is easy to compel men to do what they would not do freely if allowed an opportunity for their reason to work. The problem was to prevent the working of reason. Today, as we know, an order is issued by The Chosen, and is followed by a campaign in the Press, and by revivals exhorted from the Pulpit. There is no chance for the intrusion of reason.--No facts are ever issued for reason to work upon, no questioning is ever allowed. The suggestions of the Press and Pulpit prompt loyalty and obedience, and what might, in early times, have been resented as ridiculous, becomes the mode; and thus, if any rebels exist, it is but briefly, for they are denounced as solitary and repugnant independents. A suggestion becomes public opinion because the majority of people accept it without knowing there is reason to question the suggestion; and the minority also accept it in the end through weariness of an unpleasant and even dangerous distinction.

Yet not, observe, all the minority. It was the experience of our forefathers that unsuspected centres of infection always remained, and were not discovered till they had poisoned large areas of the country. Some bold fellow, here and there, had withstood all efforts at intimidation, and in time made others as courageous as himself. A means had to be found to eliminate the possibility of infection by original minds, or clearly the Holy State could not consider itself safe. Here, indeed, we see the hardest of the problems statesmen of the past had to solve. From the mere negation of the Censorship, a positive advance had to be made to the obliteration of original thought. This at first, necessarily, was but tentative, and only the confidence gained through successful experiment enabled governments at last to find where the real trouble lay.

It was supposed, at first, that the destruction of subversive political tracts and the persecution of radical views would be enough. Yet, of course, it was learned that as fast as these were cropped, growth elsewhere had become vigorous. The human intelligence is natively prone to look towards new things. Then it was that, after a long suspicion of the origin of ideals, great statesmen were led to an examination of classic literature and a study of the arts. Then they saw, what they might have known sooner, that in the very institutions supported by the State, the Public Libraries and Art Galleries, were actually preserved the potent ideals which demeaned that general opinion which the State was laboring to establish.

The famous Day of Release was ordered. This was ordained to free mankind from its heritage of the spirit. A test was made, and by that test any book or picture or poem which could not be approved or understood by native deacons of Solomon Island missions (who were imported for the purpose) was at once extirpated. This checked a great deal of the troublesome growth of the mind. Music, however, was strangely forgotten; and it was proved that the great revolution which burst out in Europe 120 years after the "Great War" began in the emotion occasioned by the continued playing of the compositions of one Beethoven, whose work is now fortunately lost, and other music which remained in favor in spite of the official insistence on the use of the steam saxophone for public concerts. Men, wherever they dared, insisted on having the best. And though the records were at length destroyed, the tenacious memories of a few fanatics and cranks preserved much of the old music, and that usually of the worst and most disloyal.

Here we see another step had to be taken by men in control of the State. The memory of what was classical was kept though in an ever-fading condition, and now and again some point of memory fructified to almost its original suggestive beauty in the fortuitously abnormal brain of a genius, and thus the state work of hygiene had to be done over again; for curiously enough people everywhere rose like a tide, and moved spontaneously towards these manifestations of liberty and beauty, and away from their loyalty to the God-State. A method, therefore, had to be discovered, first for obliterating what remained in the public memory of what was magical and rebellious, and then for the elimination of any possibility of original genius arising; and genius was, it was seen, first and last, the cause of all the trouble.

The destruction of all great works of art was followed, fifty years later, by the Period of Purging. All who were denounced for having quoted forbidden poetry, or for humming forbidden music, were executed. Such malefactors, who refused to forget, obviously could not be allowed to live. This gave a long period of peace, in which the Sacred Entity, the Unassailable Authority, took concrete form. Even so, the destruction of the treasures of the past, and of all memory of them, did not prevent the spontaneous appearance, now and then, of extraordinary men who, by divination it would seem, perceived a flatness and monotony in society, a sameness of common thought, and who laughed at the estimable uniform flocks; often, indeed, stampeding them.

Now science had its turn. It was more than a century since the works of Darwin and other philosophers had been burned. Young students who showed an aptitude for science, and so were potentially dangerous, were taken early within the Sacred Precincts, initiated into the mysteries of the Priests, and were given work and safety under the shadow of the Entity. They rarely went wrong; and when they did they went further or were heard of no more.

These men of science were set the problem of finding a method of sterilizing the unfit, that is, people who showed any decadent tendency to originality. All the increase of population by that time was occasioned under the direction of the High Priests, so that the Holy State had not only the power of dealing death, but of bringing new life. The new life, it is evident, had to be determined, as far as possible, by a scientific specification of a perfect citizen; and in the course of a century or two, through the destruction of intelligence wherever it inadvertently appeared, through the selection of parents sufficiently loyal and docile to accept marriage immediately when ordered by officials, and by certain signs, such as lustiness, by which, at a birth, the skilled Public Watchers who accompanied midwives were made suspicious of the new-born as possible enemies of the State, at last mankind arrived at its present perfection, content, and happiness, with hardly an intellectual doubt or a sign of suspicious joy to mar the whole serene horizon of the Holy State's exactitude.

Yet, we dare ask, had it not been for that little "War to End War" of 1914-1918, so innocently named by our forefathers who had too much liberty to know what they were talking about, would the possibility of our present social tranquility have arisen? It is hardly likely. The freedom we enjoy from all criticism, from all interruptions of mind and spirit, an internal peace which is indeed never broken except by the lethal germs of our modern wars that, in the due course of nature, obliterate every week or so a few of our cities, was a lucky chance that was seized upon by public-spirited legislators who had the prescience to know its value.

# IN VINO DEMI-TASSE
# CHARLES HANSON TOWNE

The Young-Old Philosopher and I were sitting in one of the innumerable restaurants in New York where the sanctity of the law is about as much considered as a bicycle ride up Mt. Etna. At the next table--indeed, all around us--rich red wine was being poured into little cups.

"The new motto of America should be '*In vino demi-tasse*,'" my friend said, smiling. And I quite agreed with him. For it is being done everywhere; in the most exalted circles, and in the lowest. Poor old human nature, which an organized minority are so bent upon changing overnight, cannot be altered; and, all the emphasis in a supposedly free country having been placed upon not drinking, the prohibitionists are wondering why so many of us care for liquid refreshment.

There is too much *verboten* in America today. I can remember the time, not so long ago, when no dinner-party was counted a success unless four or five cocktails were served before we sat down at the table. But that era passed. It was soon evident that such foolishness would lead to grave disaster--if not to the grave; and the young business man who was seen to consume even one glass of beer at luncheon was frowned upon, catalogued as unsteady, even in the face of the fact that perhaps the most efficient people in the world were automatic beer-drinkers.

As to drinking, in America we had other ideas. Big Business, which has become such a potent factor among us, and more a part of our national consciousness than Art and Letters ever will be, of its own volition placed a ban upon immoderate drinking; and the sane among us--of whom there were still many--gladly fell in line, and either went periodically upon the water-wagon or took a nip only occasionally when the cares of life weighed too heavily and insistently upon us.

Why, then, the Reformers? Why the Uplift Workers? Why the Extremists?

Not content with a great and wise people working out their own salvation from within, they must step forth in solemn battalions, and make us pure and holy--from without.

We resent them. There is no reason why an entire nation should be indicted for the sins and failings of a few. It would be quite as sensible to forbid connubial bliss because there are a handful of libertines in the world.

The cry goes up, however, that the next generation will be so much better because of our enforced good behavior now. I am afraid that I am not enough of an altruist to care so definitely about the morals of a race unborn. I feel that my children, looking over the files of our newspapers, as they sip their light wine and beer, may smile and say, "Poor grandpa! He had so little self-control that the Government had to put the screws on him and his friends. Too bad! They must have been a fast set in his day. And yet--he left us a pretty good heritage of health and strength. We wonder if he was such an awful devil as history makes out."

The truth is that nothing, in moderation, ever hurt anybody. That is why the wise among us are against Prohibition and strongly for Temperance. Normal men do not like to be coddled. If coddling is done, however, they like to pick their coddlers. We don't like a lean and sour-visaged Prohibitionist making a fuss over us, feeling our pulse, taking our temperature, smoothing our brow. The whole trouble with the world today, as a sane man views it, is that there has been altogether too much coddling of the physically and mentally unfit.

We have become, through drifting, a nation of hypocrites. We make laws so fast that the bewildered citizen cannot follow them. We add amendment after amendment to our Constitution, and then laugh at what we have done, the while we secretly rebel. We have few convictions, and we refuse to face issues squarely and honestly. We pretend to be virtuous before the rest of the world; but we are like the ostrich which hides its head in the sands. We pretend that, just as the eugenists think of the physical attributes of the coming generation, we consider the mental attributes--and we turn around and raise a race of bootleggers. We permit our enormous foreign population to see us at our legislative work; and then we go proudly and sanctimoniously to restaurants and allow Italian, German and French waiters to pour red wine into our demi-tasses.

Oh, we are not in our cups--only in our half-cups. It would all be very amusing were it not so terribly serious. For we are rapidly floating toward trouble; and, hypocritically enough, we will not admit it. When it is said, since the tragedy of Prohibition, that the reformers will next snatch our cigars and cigarettes out of our mouths, we shrug our shoulders, smile and pass on, saying, "Oh, no! ***that*** would be going ***too*** far!"--in the face of what already has been accomplished in this land of the spree and the home of the grave.

Yes, we have become grave indeed. For there can be no doubt that there is a feeling of great unhappiness and unrest in America now. One hears the most solid citizens saying, "I do not try to save any more; I merely live from day to day, hoping against hope that things will right themselves, and that the old order will somehow return."

Who gets a long-term lease nowadays? Those of us who are old enough to remember the simplicity and peace of the golden 'Eighties and 'Nineties are appalled at the nervous tension and complexities of this hour. We are all catalogued and tagged, just as they are in that Prussia we so recently and fervently despised; and we are hounded by income-tax investigators, surrounded by a horde of spies who search our luggage, pry into our kitchens to see if we are making home brew, raided in restaurants--and laughed at by king-ridden and shackled Europeans.

It isn't pleasant to realize that you are burdened with taxes partly to cover the salaries of Federal Officers whose delicate duty it is to spy upon you. And then when you walk out and talk to the police-man on your street, he will whisper in your ear that he knows where he can get you some delicious ale, and see to it that it is safely delivered at your door. This is the America, deny it as we will, that we are living in today. I confess that I hang my head a bit, and am ashamed to look a Frenchman in the face.

Not long ago, at a dinner, I asked a certain politician--I refuse to grace him with the name of statesman, though he has ambitions to be known as such--why, if he believed in the Volstead Act, he still consumed whiskey. His answer was intended to be amusing; to me it was disgraceful. Said he: "I am drinking as much as I can in order to lessen the supply for the other fellow."

And just a while back I went to a banquet at a country club near New York. Two policemen in uniform were sent by the local authorities to "guard the place" while much liquor was poured. These minions of the sacred law were openly served with highballs, and laughed at the Constitution of the United States, the while they drank. Everyone at that party was loud in denunciation of Prohibition and what has come in its wake, yet went on dancing with the casual remark that it was of no consequence that they broke the law, since everyone was doing it--and everyone always would.

Uphold the law, no matter what is injected into it, I have heard people cry. That, it seems to me, is mere Teutonic stupidity, and has no part in the attitude of thinking men and women in a land like America. I suppose, arguing thus, that if a law were passed tomorrow prohibiting the carrying of, say, hand-bags or canes, they would feel it incumbent upon themselves, as good Americans, to fall into line, bow the knee and whisper meekly, "All right, O most beloved country! I obey!"

A good American, as I understand it, is not one who ignorantly stands for the letter of the law, no matter what that law may be. A good American is one who tries to set his country right; one who looks beyond the present ungenerous attitude of the fanatics; one who visualizes the future and prays that our liberty may not be further jeopardized, for the good of the generations that are to follow us.

We fought to rid the world of autocracy, yet we have suddenly become the most autocratic nation on earth. Prohibition is a symbol of the death of freedom. The issue at stake is as clear-cut as taxation without representation; and our legislators should remember a certain well-known Boston tea-party. There would have been no United States of America unless a few honest men with sound convictions had rebelled and protested against tyranny. The right kind of rebel makes the right kind of citizen.

I have heard a few people liken one's duty in the matter of the draft to the Prohibition law. If we obeyed a summons to fight, whether we liked fighting or not, we should likewise obey the law regarding drinking, they contend. The two things are as separated as the Poles. In 1914, and thereafter, civilization itself was at stake; and that man would have been blind indeed who did not see the stern and clear-cut issues before us all. We leaped to arms because we wanted to protect humanity, because the death-knell of democracy was sounding. Prohibition, these same people would tell us, should be enforced to save poor, weak humanity and civilization again, and we should fight to that end. Yet as long as the world has been moving, civilized man has been consuming a certain amount of alcohol, and has been in no serious danger of going down to disaster. We have progressed through the ages, despite our cheerful cups of wine; and though of course a few imbeciles have dropped from the line, the rest of us have been none the worse--in fact, sometimes a little better--for our occasional libations. Let anyone deny this who has ever, for a moment even, been in Arcady! And the dreadful and incontrovertible fact remains that the sober nations have not proved themselves superior to those who drink in moderation.

Who are happy over Prohibition? First, the Prohibitionists themselves, and, secondly, the bootleggers. The more the lid is clamped on in our great cities, the more rejoicing goes on in that mysterious inner and under circle which dispenses liquor, and will continue to dispense it, I fear, until the end of time. Whenever there is a "drive" on in New York to "mop up the place," prices soar to the skies, and the illicit trade waxes brisker than ever. No wonder the bootleggers grow happy--and rich; and evade the income tax which the rest of us must pay.

I am not sympathetic toward those who say that they have been driven to excessive drinking because a certain obnoxious law has been passed. The only way to fight Prohibition is to fight it soberly; it is the jingled and jangled arguments of barroom bores that hurt the cause of the men and women who are moderate drinkers, and who wish with all their hearts to see a return to common sense in our country.

We Americans never do anything piecemeal. Probably at the root of all our strange fanaticism about drink was the thought that the saloon had better go; that it was time for such foul places to disappear. The pendulum had to swing all the way. If it would swing back a little; if the Government would step in and control the liquor traffic, do away with spirits, except for medicinal purposes, and give the people light wine and beer, a truce could be declared over night. Drunkenness should be made a prison offence. No matter who the offender against public decency is he should be lodged in jail. Whether one is a so-called gentleman coming out of his club, or the meanest tramp in the streets, he should be punished. There would be no visible drunkenness if a law like this were passed and rigorously enforced.

I am afraid that so long as grapes grow on vines and apples on trees; so long as fermentation is one of Nature's processes, there can be no such thing as Prohibition. And the Biblical justification for drinking is pleasant reading for those who like, now and then, a little wine at their dinner tables. Yet there are fanatics who rise up and shout that the wine Christ caused to appear at the marriage feast of Cana was not intoxicating. What divination is theirs which makes them so positive? If water was just as good, why did not water remain in the casks?

If we would spend more time making laws that worked for good, rather than for evil--and Graft is a great evil; if we would realize that it is not so much our concern to make the other fellow good as to make him happy, as Stevenson so beautifully puts it--then, I say, we would be better employed than we are today with our foolish, fussy bills and acts, mandates, precepts and restrictions.

I believe firmly in local option in all things; but there is no reason why New York, or any other great city, should live as Kansas and Idaho live. I prefer New York because a big city gives me a spiritual uplift that a prairie town does not. It is my privilege to live where I desire. I like to hear fine music, to come in contact with intellectuals; to go to plays that are worth while; to read books that satisfy my soul. I find such a life in New York. I have no quarrel with the man who prefers the silence and loneliness of forests and plains. He may be far happier than I. But I do insist that if I let him alone, he also should let me alone. Throbbing cities thrill me: cities with their glamour, their wonder, their enchantment, their dreams of agate and stone, their lofty towers that plunge to the very skies and kiss the clouds. I happen to like the innocent laughter in a glass of champagne. You may call it wicked hilarity. But the Continental manner of living appeals to me. I like the color and warmth and fervor of life; and people who drink red wine with their meals seem to me to be more cosmopolitan than those who do not. All this seems part of the pageant of life to me. I am not provincial, and I do not care to be made provincial by unintelligent and unimaginative law-makers.

It may be that I am entirely wrong. I do not know. But I do know that it seems utterly unreasonable to force me to abstain from wine if I wish it, just because there are a few heavy imbibers of whiskey in the world. I think it is a far more serious matter to have practically all of us law-breakers than to have one-half of one per cent of us drunkards.

Let us have done with insincere, inelastic laws, and get back to wisdom and truth and sanity.

# BOOTLEG
# JOHN V. A. WEAVER

(With a graceful bow to Don Marquis)

You heard me! How many times I got to tell you?
Them is my words: you leave that girl alone.
Leave her alone, you hear? Leave her alone!
You think I'll have my son foolin' around
A little snippy rat that's all stuck-up,
And thinks my son's not good enough for her?
"Yeh," that's what Bill says, "Yeh, it's like I say;
Ellen is got swell friends up on the Drive;
I'm sorry she had to break a date with Fred.
But still, you know, the world is changed a lot,
And we changed with it. You're about the same,
But me--well, I been gettin' right along,
And honest, Jack, you see the sense yourself--
Why should I let my daughter marry a clerk?"

Can you believe it? Why, I damn near fainted.
His daughter too good for the likes of us!
Of course I got so mad I couldn't see!
Of course I pasted him square in the eye!
And if I catch him sayin' things about me
I'll knock his stuck-up head off! And I tell you,

If you go near the dirty oilcan's place,
And crawl around that snippy brat of his,
I'll kick you out into the street to stay.
You hear that? Eight out in the street you go!
The nerve! The dirty, lousy, low-down crook!
A Bootleg gettin' stuck-up over money!
The world is crazy, that's all there is to it!
Crazy, I tell you! All turned upside-down!

Listen. It's fifteen years I know this Bill.
Them good old days, most every afternoon
On the way home from the lumber yards I'd drop in
And get a beer, and gas around a while.
That was my second home, I useta say,
And Bill's Place was a home you could be proud of.
Say. The old woman never kep' a floor
As clean as Bill's was. And the brass spittoons
And rail-you could of shaved lookin' in one.
And all the glasses polished! And the tables
So neat! And over at the free-lunch counter,
Charlie the coon with a apron white like chalk,
Dishin' out hot-dogs, and them Boston Beans,
And Sad'dy nights a great big hot roast ham,
Or roast beef simply yellin' to be et,
And washed down with a seidel of old Schlitz!

Oh, say, that sure was fun, and don't forget it.
Old Ed, and Tom, and Baldy Frank McGee,
And the two Bentleys, we was all the reg'lars.
It was our meetin'-place. And there we stood,
And Lord! The rows about the government,
And arguin! and all about the country,
How it was goin' to the dogs. And maybe

Somebody'd start a song, and old Pop Dikes
Would have to quit the checker-game in the corner
That him and Fat Connell was always playin',
And never gettin' through. I never seen

No bums come in and stay for more'n a minute;
Bill didn't like to have no drunks around;
He made 'em hit the air. Well, some of us,
Of course, might get just a wee mite too much
Under the belt, but who did that ever hurt?
At least we knowed the licker wasn't poison.
And when somebody would get very lit
Bill was right there to try and make him stop;
I can't see how it ever hurt us any.

And Bill! He was some barkeep! One swell guy!
A pleasant word for everybody, always,
Straight as a string, and just the whole world's friend.
I never saw a guy was liked so much.
He hardly took a drink, just a cigar,
And oncet a while a pony, say, of lager.
And my, the way that bird could tell a story!
Why, many a time I laughed until I cried.
And if it happened I was out of dough,
Bill was right there to make a little loan.
Generous, that was Bill, and one good pal.
A great old place it was, that place of Bill's.
Them was the happy days!-them was the days.

I never will forget that good-bye party
The night that Prohibition was wished on us.
You bet it wasn't any rough-house then.
We all stood 'round the bar, solemn and quiet,

And couldn't hardly think of what to say.
Bill--it was funny what had happened to him.
He didn't crack a smile the whole blame night.
He just would shake his head, and bite his lips,
And gosh, the way his eyes was shootin' fire.
The last thing that he said before I left,
"By God, I'll get back at 'em, you just wait!
I'm closing here. But don't you fret--I'll get 'em--
The dirty, pussy-footin' lousy skunks!"

I had to go home early. And the next day
I seen the wagons comin' to take the bar
And all the furniture. I felt like cryin'.

Well, you know what this prohibition is.

Bill goes away, and stays about three months.
And then one day I meets him on the street.
"Well, Jack," he says, "You want some real good gin?"
"Just what I need," I says. "All right," he says,
"You come down to the house at nine o'clock.
I'll fix you up. I'll give you half a case
Four Bucks a bottle."... "Four a bottle!" I says,
Thinkin' he must be kiddin'. "Sure," he says,
"I got to make my profit. There's the risk.
This is good stuff. I made it by myself.
I guarantee that it won't make you sick."
"I'm sick already, just from hearin' the price.
No thanks. Not now," I says. He says all right,
But when I want some, just remember him.

And so, of course, later I did want some,
And had to pay that much, and even more;

But hell, what can you do? So long's you're sure
The stuff ain't goin' to burn your insides out,
You got to pay the price. And all the friends
That Bill had useta have is customers,

And all get stung the same. And dozens more.
Them old days Bill was one fine friend for sure,
Happy and nice and straight and generous.
And now to think he high-brows you and me!
A great big house he's got, and a new Packard,
And di'monds for his wife, that scrubbed the floors
Back in the days when he was only barkeep.
That's what this Prohibition done for him,
And what's it do for me, I'd like to know?
It makes a crook of me, the same as him,
Only I'm losin' money, and he gets it.
Why, say, I catch myself all of the time
Laughin' about this Prohibition law,
And figgerin' new ways how I could break it.
And that's the way it is with everybody.
We get to see that one law is a joke,
And think it's smart to bust it all to pieces.
And pretty soon there's all the other laws,
And how're you goin' to keep from think' likewise
About a thing like stealin', and all that?
No wonder that we got these here now crime waves!
No wonder everybody is a crook!

But that ain't what I'm sayin' to you now!
You leave that stuck-up little Jane alone!
They's plenty of girls that's pretty in the world--
You leave that dirty oilcan's daughter be.
Ten years ago she used to run around

And rush the can for me and other folks.
Now she's a real swell lady! Damn her eyes,
And Bill's, and them there pussy-footin' fish!
The world is, crazy! And I'm goin' nuts!
High-tonin' me! You hear me? If I catch you
Foolin' around that girl, I kick you out,
So fast you won't know what has ever hit you!

A bootleg's daughter! Hell!

# AND THE PLAYWRIGHT
# ALEXANDER WOOLLCOTT

Every American playwright goes about his work these days oppressed by a foreboding. He suspects that before long a censor is going to materialize out of thin air to take stern and morose charge of the American theatre. It is true that no statutory precipitation of such an agent has been definitely proposed. It is true that the policeman from the nearest corner has not gone so far as to drop around and warn him that he'd better be careful. Nevertheless, he has the foreboding. He perceives dimly that a desire to chasten the stage is in the air. And he is right. It, is. It has been ever since the war.

Of course an itch to lay hands on the theatre was begetting restlessness in the American bosom considerably prior to April 6, 1917. It is part of this country's Puritan inheritance to believe that playgoing is somehow bad, that an enjoyment and patronage of the theatre is sinful. This belief flows as an unconscious undercurrent in the thought even of those clergymen who try pathetically hard to seem and be liberal and unpharisaical, the kind who always begin their lectures on Avery Hopwood by saying that they yield to no one in their admiration and respect for the many splendid ladies and gentlemen of the stage whom they are proud to number among their acquaintances.

Shaw, in his comparatively mild-mannered preface to "The Showing Up of Blanco Posnet," recognizes the Puritan hostility to the theatre, but, somewhat perversely, ascribes it to the fact that the *promenoirs* have always been used as show-windows by the courtesans of each generation. I suspect, however, that that hostility was more deeply rooted. The Puritans disliked the theatre because it was jolly. It was a place where people went in deliberate quest of enjoyment. And you weren't supposed to do that on earth. Plenty of time for that later on.

When I was a knee-breeched schoolboy in Philadelphia, some of the more dissipated of us used to organize Saturday excursions to Keith's old Eighth Street Theatre, a vaudeville temple known to the natives as the Buy-Joe. Fortified with a quarter and some sandwiches, one went at eleven in the morning and hung on till the edge of midnight. To my genuine surprise and confusion, I gathered that some of our classmates not only avoided these orgies, but sincerely believed that we, who indulged in them were simply courting Hell's fire. They stayed at home and, I suppose, read "Elsie Dinsmore."

It so happens that I never encountered that book during my formative years, but was in my hopelessly corrupted thirties before ever I saw a copy. Even then, it did not lack interest. And one passage, at least, richly rewarded a glance through its pages. It seems that Elsie, arriving from somewhere, reached some city in the late evening. Her father (a rakish, devil-may-care fellow who thought it was all right for Elsie to play the piano on Sunday) met her at the station and engaged a cabriolet to take her across town to whatever shelter had been selected for the night. As they were bowling along one of the principal streets, Elsie noticed a building which the author described in shuddering accents as having, if I remember correctly, "a lighted façade." The tone, if not the precise words of the description, rather suggested that here was a gambling hell whose lower circles were dedicated to rites of nameless infamy. Elsie shrank back into the cloistered shadows of the cab. "Oh, father," she cried in hurt bewilderment, "what kind of place was that?" Smitten, apparently, with a certain remorse that he had suffered her virginal eyes to reflect so scabrous a spot, he put a sheltering arm around her and said, sadly: "That, little daughter, was a THEATRE."

At which limp climax, perhaps, you smile a little. But it is well to remember that the children who were molded by "Elsie Dinsmore" are now grown up and can be detected voting warmly at every election. Many of them kicked over the traces long ago, but there are also many who are reading Harold Bell Wright today. They admire Henry Ford. They sit enthralled at the feet of Dr. John Roach Straton. And, not wryly but with undiscouraged faith, they vote away for the Hylans and the Hardings of each recurrent crisis. They brought the bootlegger into existence and, at a rallying cry lifted by anyone against the theatre, they will come scurrying intently from a thousand unsuspected flats and two-story houses.

They are the more responsive to such cries since the war. That might have been foreseen by any one at all familiar with the psychopathology of reform. A cigarette addict who, in a spartan moment, swears off smoking, is familiar enough with the inner gnaw that robs him of his sleep and roils his dinner for days and days. His body, long habituated to the tobacco, had dutifully taken on the business of manufacturing its antidote. When the tobacco is abruptly removed, the body continues for a while to turn out the antidote as usual and during that while, that antidote goes roaming angrily through the system, seeking something to oppose and destroy.

A somewhat analogous condition has agitated the body politic ever since the late Fall of 1918. The passage of the Eighteenth Amendment had robbed the prohibitionists of their chief excitement; then the signing of the Armistice took away the glamor of public-spiritedness from all those good people who had had such a splendid time keeping an eye on their presumably treasonable neighbors. Behold, then, the Busy Body (which is in every one of us) all dressed up and nowhere to go. The itch became tremendous. The moving pictures caught it first. No wonder the American playwright is uneasy. He ought to be.

He dreads a censorship of the theatre because he suspects (not without reason) that it will be corrupt, that it will work foolishly, and that, having taken and relished an inch, it will take an ell.

He is the more uneasy because he realizes that the theatre presents a special incitement and a special problem--a problem altogether different from that presented by the bookstall, for instance. The play, once produced, is open to all the world. It may have been written with the thought that it would amuse Franklin P. Adams, but it is attended (in a body) by the Unintelligentsia. It may have been heavily seasoned in the hope that it would jounce the rough boy of Baltimore, H. L. Mencken-and lo, there in the third row on the aisle, is Dr. Frank Crane, being made visibly ill by it. Your playwright may write a piece to touch the memories and stir the hearts of elderly sinners, but he has to face the fact that the girls from Miss Spence's school may come fluttering to it, row on row.

On his desk is a seductive two-volume assemblage of "Poetica Erotica," edited by T. R. Smith, the antiquarian. It is a book which, if flaunted, would agitate the Postmaster General, stir up the Grand Jury, and make the Society for the Suppression of Vice call a special mass-meeting. It is managed as a commercial article by a system of furtive, semi-private sales which probably enhance its value as a source of revenue and yet shut the mouth of the heirs of Anthony Comstock. A folder announces that the juicy Satyr icon of Petronius Arbiter will shortly issue from the same presses. And so on, endlessly. It is a neat arrangement but one which cannot be imitated by the playwright. When he wants to be naughty, he must make up his mind to being naughty right out on the street-corner where every one can see him.

And though, in the moments when he is disposed to temporize, he sometimes thinks that suspect plays might, like saucy novels, be first inspected in manuscript, he knows full well that no such tactics are really feasible in the theatre. Your publisher, inwardly hot with resentment, may nevertheless take the occasional precaution of showing the script of a thin-ice book to the authorities--even to the self-constituted ones--thereby forestalling prosecution by agreeing to delete in advance such phrases and incidents as seem likely to agitate those authorities unduly. But the flavor and significance of a play depends too much on the manner of its performance and cannot be clearly forecast prior to that performance any more than the hue of a goblet can be guessed before the wine is poured. I can testify to that--I, who in my time, have seen players make a minx out of Ophelia, a mild-mannered mouse out of Katherine, an honest woman out of Lady Macbeth and a benevolent old gentleman out of Shylock. I have seen French players cast as the servants of Petruchio invade "The Taming of the Shrew" with a comic pantomime in which they fought for their turns at the keyhole of Petruchio's bedroom wherein Kate was being subjected to a little off-stage taming. It would have amused Shakespeare immoderately, I imagine, and certainly it would have surprised him. Until his piece is spoken, even the author cannot tell--and thereafter, from night to night, he cannot be sure.

That is why there is the quality of an eternal fable in the pathetic old tale of the stagehand who had always felt that, if chance would ever give him even the smallest of rôles, he would show these actors where their shortcomings were. He would not drone out even the least important and most perfunctory of speeches. Not he. Into every syllable he would pour real meaning, real conviction. At last, after twenty years of yearning from the wings, chance did rush him on as an understudy. Unfortunately, he was assigned to the role of the page in "King John," who must march into the throne-room and announce the approach of Philip the Bastard.

So, it seems apparent that any real supervision of the theatre must function with relation to produced plays and cannot deal with mere unembodied and undetermined manuscripts.

Our playwright's suspicion that such supervision, if managed by a politically appointed censor, would work foolishly, are justified by all he has heard of such functionaries as they have worked in other fields and in other lands. This was true of the gag which the doughty Brieux finally pried off the mouth of the French playwright. It has certainly been true of the mild and intermittent discipline to which the remote and slightly puzzled Lord Chamberlain has subjected the English dramatists. Indeed, when their mutinous mutterings finally jogged Parliament into inspecting his activities, the Lord Chamberlain was somewhat taken aback by the tactics of Shaw, who, instead of hissing him for forbidding public performances of certain Shaw and Ibsen plays, derided and denounced him instead for the plays he had *not* suppressed. And indeed, for every play which the Lord Chamberlain has suppressed, the old playgoer of London could point to five which, had he been more intelligent, he might more reasonably have suppressed in its place.

But after all those scuffles on the Strand do seem part of the strange customs of a fusty-dusty never-never land. So our American playwright turns, instead, to the purifications effected nearer home. He looks apprehensively into the matter of the movies. As an occasional scenario writer, he has been instructed by bulletins sent out for his guidance, little watch-your-step leaflets which list the alterations ordered in earlier pictures by the august Motion Picture Commission of the State of New York. Most of them are fussy little disapprovals of language used in the titles. You mustn't say: "I shall kill Lester Crope." Better say: "I shall destroy the false Lester Crope" or something like that. You mustn't say "roué." You mustn't say: "I don't like that rich old roué hanging around you." Better say: "I don't like that rich old sport." And when, in a moment of self-indulgence, a title-writer allowed himself the luxury of writing "In a moment of madness, I wronged a woman," the Censor seems to have turned scarlet and issued the following order: "Substitute for 'wronged' the word 'offended' or something similar."

"Or something similar." Somehow, that seems to recall an old "Spanish for Beginners" textbook which bade me not bother with the "tutoyer" business as it would not be needed during my travels in Spain, unless I married there "or something similar."

At all events, no playwright can be scoffed at as an alarmist who ventures to fear that a censorship of the drama will, in practice, be foolish. At the thought of such frivolous and fatuous blue-pencillings of his next drama (which is to be his master-piece, by the way) our playwright becomes profoundly depressed and every time he goes out to dinner or finds himself with a small, cornered audience at the club, he winds up the talk on this bugaboo of his.

Out of the resulting prattle, two widespread impressions always come to the top, two familiar comments on the subject which, whenever questionable plays are mentioned, seem to emerge as regularly and as automatically as does the applause which follows the rendition of Dixie by any restaurant orchestra in New York. Both comments are absurd.

One comes from the man who can be counted on to say: "They tell me that show at the Eltinge--What's it called? 'Tickling Tottie's Tummy?'--well, they say it's pretty raw. Certainly does beat all how there are some men who just have to see a show soon's they hear it's smutty. I can't understand it."

This might be called the Comment Ingenuous. A man who never fails to edge into any group whence the bent head and the hoarse chuckle tells him that a shady story is on, a man who would have to think hard to name a friend of his to whom he would not rush with the latest scandalous anecdote brought in by the drummers from Utica--such a man will, nevertheless, express a pious surprise when the crowds flock to see the latest Hopwood farce just because it is advertised as indecorous. It is not known why he is surprised.

Or, if he is not surprised, then he falls over backward and makes the Comment Cynical. When he hears that "Under Betty's Bolster" is making a fortune while "The Grey Iconoclast" is playing to empty benches next door, he gives a sardonic little laugh (which he reserves for just such occasions) and says: "Of course. You might have known. Old Channing Pollock was right when he said: 'Nothing risqué, nothing gained.' Don't the smutty shows always make money? Doesn't the public invariably stampede to the most bedridden plays? Isn't the pornographic play the most valuable of all theatrical properties?"

To which rhetorical questions, the answer in each case, as it happens, is "No." The blush is not, of course, a bad sign in the box-office. But the chuckle of recognition is a better one. So is the glow of sentiment. So is the tear of sympathy. The smutty and the scandalous have a smaller and less active market than homely humor, for instance, or melodramatic excitement or pretty sentiment. When "Aphrodite" was brought here from Paris, it was, for various reasons, impossible to recapture for the translated dramatization the flavor of abnormal eroticism which lent the book a certain phosphorescent glow at home. So its producers relied on lots and lots of nudity to give it réclame here. At this the Hearst papers did some rather pointed blushing and the next morning, there was a grand scrimmage at the box-office and seats were hawked about for grotesque prices. Whereupon the Comment Cynical could be heard on all sides. But when at the end of the season or so later, "Aphrodite" was withdrawn with a shortage of a hundred and ninety thousand dollars or so on its books, the Cynics were too engrossed with some other play to mention the fact. To be sure that shortage was more than made up next season on the road, but it ought to be mentioned that "Aphrodite" knew the indignity of many and many an empty row in New York.

The great fortunes, as a matter of fact, are made with plays like "Peg o' My Heart" and "The First Year," both as pure as the driven snow. It is true that Avery Hopwood has grown rich on his royalties. But not so rich as Winchell Smith, who has dealt exclusively with sweetness and light. Also those who laugh most caustically over the Hopwood estate usually find it convenient to ignore the fact that the greatest single contribution to it has been made by "The Bat," at which Dr. Straton might conceivably faint from excitement but at which he would have to work pretty hard to do any blushing.

So much for the familiar catch-words and their validity. A little discouraged by the fatuity of all lay discussion, our playwright may be pictured as retreating to the clubrooms of the American Dramatists and there finding his fellow-craftsmen all busy as bees on scenarios overflowing with not particularly original sin. They are turning them out hurriedly with an "After-me-the-deluge" gleam in their haunted eyes. Some such despairing courtship of disaster may be needed to explain the jostling procession of harlots which marked the American Drama in the season of 1921-1922. An unprecedentedly large percentage of the heroines had either just been ruined (or were just about to be ruined) as the first curtain rose. Also the plays wallowed in a defiant squalor of language which, five years before, would have called out the reserves.

The privilege to indulge in such didos is not, as a matter of fact, especially dear to them. They do not really prize unduly the right to use the word "slut" once in every act. They can even bear up whenever a law forbids disrobing on the stage. They know that most pruriency in the theatre derives from the old frustrations sealed up and festering in the mind of the onlooker who detects it. They suspect, from what little reading they have managed in the psychology of outlets, that the more mock-raping there is done on the stage of the local opera house, the less real raping will be done on the greensward of the nearest park. But they know, too, that the force of modesty is one of the strongest and most ancient instincts of civilized man, that probably it is a sound and healthy one, inextricably involved in the race's instinct of self-preservation and self-perpetuation. Anyway, they feel that the discussion draws them into matters unarguable.

They dread a Censor most for fear his appetite will grow by what it feeds on. They know that the Lord Chamberlain began by exorcising obscenity from the English theatre and ended by banning so fiercely Puritanical a play as "Mrs. Warren's Profession" because it admitted the existence of brothel-keeping as a business and by shutting up such innocent merriment as "The Mikado" because its jocularity might offend the (at the moment) dear Japanese.

Most American playwrights would derive a certain enjoyment from watching a posse of citizens in wrathful pursuit of one of those theatrical managers who are big brothers to the trembling crones that totter up to you on the *Boulevard des Italiens* and try to sell you a few obscene postal-cards. But most American playwrights would feel a genuine apprehension lest such a posse, confused in its values and its mission, might then turn and lock up Eugene O'Neill because of the rough talk that lends veracity to "The Hairy Ape" or because of the steady scrutiny which has the effect of stripping naked the unhappy creatures of his play called "Diff'rent."

They would be perfectly willing to co-operate with a State official appointed to prevent the use of naughty words on the American stage, but they darkly suspect that he would then require every heroine to bring a letter from her pastor and would end by interfering with all plays which suggested, for instance, that government had been known, from time to time, to prove corrupt, wealth to become oppressive and law, on rare occasions, to seem just a wee bit unjust. They are minded to resist any supervision of the theatre's manners for fear it might shackle in time the theatre's thought. Today or tomorrow they may be seen temporizing or at least negotiating with the forces of suppression in any community, but they are really seeking all the time to frustrate those forces. And will so seek ever and always, law or no law. It was just such frustration they were seeking when after a season of ruined heroines (and ruined managers) they all gravely sat down in April, 1922, and drew up a panel of 300 pure-minded citizens from which a jury could be called to pass on any play complained of.

And they have the comfort of knowing that any such supervision, today or tomorrow, legalized or roundabout, mild or incessant, is bound to be superficial, spasmodic and largely formal. They know that in the long run the theatre in each day and community, will manage somehow to express the taste of that day and community. They know that it is among the sweet revenges of life that the o'er-leaping censor always defeats himself.

They derive a curious comfort from the story of the reviewer for a Boston journal who once described a musician as remaining seated through a concert in the pensive attitude of Buddha contemplating his navel. It is a story within whose implications lies all that has ever been said, or ever will be said, about censorship. The copy-readers and make-up men, it seems, could see nothing especially infamous in their reviewer's little simile. As poor George Sampson said of the outraged Mrs. Wilfer's under-petticoat: "We know it's there." At all events, the offending word passed all the sentries and was printed as written, when, too late, it caught the horrified eye of the proprietor. At the sight of so crassly physical a term in the chaste columns of his own paper, he rushed to the telephone at the club and called up the managing editor. That word must come out. But the paper was already on the presses. Even as they spoke, these were whirling out copy after copy. Too late to reset? Yes, much too late. But was there not still some remedy which would keep at least part of the edition free from that dreadful word? Wasn't it still possible to rout out the type at that point, to chisel the word away and leave a blank? Yes, that was possible. So the presses were halted, the one word was scraped out, the presses whirred again and the review, with a gape in the line, went up and down Beacon Street. Whereat Boston that night shook with a mighty laughter--the contented laughter of the unregenerate.

THE ORACLE THAT ALWAYS SAYS "NO"
THE AUTHOR OF "THE MIRRORS OF WASHINGTON"

Has anyone ever stopped to think what the nonsenseorship would do to our suppressed desires? A little while ago suppressed desires were one's own affair. One fondled them in the skeleton closet of his consciousness and was as proud of them as anyone with a haunted house is of his right, title and interest in a ghost.

They proved to him that though he went to church on Sunday and was respectably married to only one woman, he was really beneath his correct exterior a whale of a fellow, who might have been, had he but let himself go, a Casanova or at least a Byron. He patted himself on the back for keeping unruly instincts in subjection. He applauded himself for what he might be and for what he was. He got it coming and going. It was a pleasant age.

But now is he permitted to have his own secret museum of virility? I speak only of the sex which has my deepest sympathy.

No. The nonsenseorship regards him with suspicion. He must go and have even that part of him which lies below the level of his consciousness dragged forth by experts in the interests of society, and if there is anything hidden in him which might not be exhibited on the movie screens, he must have it sublimated. He cannot even have suppressed desires. He cannot be a devil of a fellow even to himself. He cannot be his own censor any longer, he must submit himself to outside censoring, to the nonsenseorship.

It all came about this way. First to establish divine right somewhere in modern government, the doctrine was set up that the public mind was infallible. Thereafter, naturally, attention centered on the public mind. What was it that it had this wonderful quality of always being right? Experience showed that it was not a thinking mind. Since it was not, then the thinking mind was anti-social.

Then our very best American philosophers, and some French ones, for the support of mass opinion, developed a system which set forth that reason always led you into traps and that the only mind to trust was the irrational, instinctive or intuitional mind. Thus the nonsenseorship, with excellent philosophic support put the ban upon thinking. Now, I do not contend that many suffer seriously from this restriction. For, after all, thinking is hard work and may cheerfully be foregone in the general interest.

But does the nonsenseorship rest content with its achievement? If the instinctive part of us is so important, let us have a look at it, says society; perhaps something anti-social may be unearthed there. A Viennese explores this area of the mind. He discovers what society would forbid, merely hidden away. Civilization has merely pressed it into dark corners, as the law has crowded the blackjack artist into alleys and dens of thieves. The psychic police are put on our trail. They must nab every suppressed desire and send it to the reform school for re-education into something beautiful and serviceable. We may not be unhappy, neurotic, mad; our complexes must be inspected. We must suppress our reason, we may not suppress our desire; the nonsenseorship says so, and to persuade us, its experts offer us the reward of health and greater usefulness if we make this further surrender.

Now, although as I have said we let reason go at the behest of the nonsenseorship without so much as a word of protest, we do not give up our suppressed desires so easily and without a fight.

As a result we see the nonsenseorship in a new light. We feel it more keenly now than ever before. It is revealed as the Procrustean bed which cramps us up until we ache inside. If there is anything the matter with us, if we are introverted, introspective, neurotic, complicated, have too much ego or too little ego, are dyspeptic, sick, sore, inhibited, regressive, defeated or too successful, unhappy, cruel or too kind, if we differ ever so slightly from the enforced average, it is because censorship presses upon us. And the cure for censorship is more censorship. Have your psychic insides censored; if you would be a perfect 36 mentally and morally, with the Hart, Schaffner & Marxed soul which modern society wills that you shall have, conform not only without but within, and be "splendidly null"! I think it is the sudden realization that just a little more of individuality, our hidden individuality, is threatened, which makes the nonsenseorship irk us now as it never did before.

The race has always had it, but in the beginning it was a crude and simple thing, troubling itself only with externals. A woman whose official duty it is to look after the virtue of the movies in Pennsylvania or Ohio, will not permit on the screen any suggestion that there is a physiological relation between a mother and a child. This method of protecting the race has its roots back in the primitive mind of mankind. When men really did not understand how children came about, births were catastrophic. A woman at a certain moment had to disappear into the wilderness; she came back having found a baby under a cabbage leaf. Any contact with her while she was making her discovery might bring pestilence and death to the tribe.

We still believe in the pestilence even if we no longer have faith in the cabbage leaf. The lady censor of Ohio or Pennsylvania is the tribe driving the pregnant woman into the wilderness. On the whole the tribe did it better than we do; it only removed the offender and the mental life of the little community went on just as before. We keep the offender amongst us and close our minds. Our simple ancestors covered no more with the fig leaf than they thought it necessary to hide; we wear the fig leaf over our eyes: that is the nonsenseorship.

Mr. Griffith recently brought out a cinema spectacle called "Orphans in the Storm," which presented many scenes from the French Revolution. Now it was not long ago that we Americans were all rather proud of the French Revolution. We had had a revolution of our own and we thought with satisfaction that the French had caught theirs from us. We were as pleased about it as the little boy is when the neighbor's little boy catches the mumps from him. He sees an enlargement of his ego in the swollen neck of his playmate.

All that is changed now. Mr. Griffith picturing the triumphant mob in Paris had to fill his screens with preachments against Bolshevism, which had as much to do with his subject as captions about the rape of the Sabine woman would have had to do with it. It is as if the little boy had been taught to believe that by never saying the word mumps, he could save his playmate from tumefying glands.

Soon some committee of morons which attends to the keeping of our intellects on the level with their own will exclude from the schools all histories which contain the words "the American Revolution." We must call it the War for American Independence. That is putting the fig leaf over our eyes. That is the nonsenseorship.

But before we decide whether or not we shall refuse to yield up our suppressed desires as we have surrendered our reason to it, with the approval of our leading philosopher, Mr. William James, let us consider some of the advantages of the nonsenseorship. Perhaps it will prove worth while to give up this little internal privilege.

First there is the simplicity of consulting the so-called public mind. The favorite aphorism of the politician and his friend and spokesman the editor is: "The public is always right upon a moral issue." This means that if the politician or the propagandist can present a question to the people in such a way that he can win his end by having the public respond in the negative, he is sure of success. It is as if society depended for its guidance upon the word of an oracle, a great stone image, out of which the priests had only succeeded in producing one response, a sound very much like, "No." The trick would consist of so framing your question that the word "no" would give you approval for your designs. That is the art of laying before the public a "moral issue" upon which it is inevitably right.

Suppose, in a society ruled by the stone image, you wanted to make war upon your neighbor. You would frame your question thus: "Shall we stand by idly and pusillanimously while our neighbor invades our land and rapes our women?" This is a moral issue of the deepest sanctity. You would present it. The priests would do their little something somewhere out of sight. From the great stone image would come a bellow which resembled "No." You would have won on a moral issue and would then be licensed to invade your neighbor's territory and rape his women.

Now you will perceive certain advantages in an oracle which can only say one word. You know in advance what its answer will be. Suppose the great stone image could have said either "yes" or "no." Suppose its answer had been "yes" to your righteous question? It would have been embarrassing. You could no longer say with such perfect confidence, "It is always right upon a moral issue."

Suppose you were capital and you desired to reduce wages. You would not go to the temple and say, "Shall we reduce wages?" That would not be a moral issue upon which the answer would be right. You would ask, "Shall we tamely acquiesce while the labor unions import the Russian revolution into our very midst?" The great stone voice always to be trusted on moral issues would thunder, "No."

Or suppose you were labor; for my oracle is even-handed--and you wished to extend your organization--you would go to the temple and propound the inquiry, "Shall we be eaten alive by the war profiteers?" The always moral voice would at least whisper "No"

It will be observed that in consulting the oracle whose answer is known in advance, the only skill required consists in so framing the question that you will get a louder roar of "no" than the other side can with its question. If you can always do this you can say with perfect confidence that old granite lungs "is always right upon a moral issue."

That is the art of being a great popular leader.

Would anyone exchange a voice like that as a ruler for the wisdom of the world's ten wisest men? We laugh at the Greeks for their practice of consulting the oracle at Delphi and rightly, for our oracle beats theirs which used to hedge in its answers and leave them in doubt. Ours never equivocates; we know its answer beforehand, for the public mind is compounded of prejudices, fears, herd instincts, youthful hatred of novelty, all easily calculable.

It has been my duty for many years to tell what public opinion is on many subjects. My method, more or less unconscious, has been to say to myself, "The public is made up largely of the unthinking. Such and such misinformation has been presented to it. Such and such prejudices and fears have been aroused. Its answer is invariably negative. The result is so and so." It is thus that judges of public opinion invariably proceed. They do not find the popular will reflected in the newspapers. They know it as a chemist knows a reaction, from familiarity with the elements combined. At least such a mind is highly convenient.

And after all who does make the best censor, or nonsenseor or whatever you choose to call it? Was it not written, "The child is censor to the man?" Well, if it was not it ought to have been, and it is now. Consider the child as it arrives in the family. Forthwith there is not merely the One Subject which may never be mentioned. There are a hundred subjects. A guard is upon the lips. The little ears must be kept pure.

Now, when we set up the establishment of democracy we did take a child into our household. I have discussed elsewhere[2] the parentage of this infant born of Rousseau and Thérèse, his moron mistress. The public mind is a child mind because in the first place the mob mind of men is primitive, youthful and undeveloped, and again because by the wide diffusion of primary instruction, we have steadily increased the number of persons with less than adult mentality who contribute to the forming of public opinion. In the nature of the case, fifty per cent. of the public must be sub-normal, that is, youthful mentality. We have reached down to the level of nonsense for our guide. That is why we call it in this book the nonsenseorship.

Every one who has watched the growth of a child's vocabulary has observed that it learns to say "no," many months, perhaps more than a year, before it ever

---

2   Chapter V, *Behind the Mirrors*

says "yes." An infant which took to saying "yes" before it did "no" would violate all precedents, would scandalize its parents, and would grow up to be a revolutionist. It would have an attitude toward life with which men should not be born and which parents and society would find subversive. On the instinct for saying "no" rests all our institutions, from the family to the state. It should exhibit itself early and become a confirmed habit before the dangerous "yes" emerges.

Besides, the child needs to say "no" long before it needs to say "yes." Foolish parents feed it mentally as they feed it physically, out of a bottle. If it had not its automatic facility of regurgitation, both mental and physical, it would suffer from excesses. Its "no" is its mental throwing up.

The public mind is still in the no-saying, the mental regurgitative stage. But is not that ideal for the nonsenseorship? Does a censor ever have need of any other word but "no"?

I have now established the convenience of an oracle whose answer "no" can always be foreseen; and the fitness of the child mind for saying "no," as well as the perfect adaptation of the single word vocabulary to the purposes of the nonsenseorship.

One of the important ends which a "no" always serves is maintaining the *status quo*. We all cling precariously to a whirling planet. We hate change for fear of somehow being spilled off into space. The nonsenseorship of the child mind is splendidly conservative. The baby in the habit of receiving its bottle from its nurse will go hungry rather than take it from its mother or father. Gilbert was wrong. Every child is not born a little radical or a little conservative.

Reaching down for the child mind in society, with some misgivings, we have been delighted to find it the strongest force making for stability. An amusing thing happened when Mr. Hearst some years ago sought readers in a lower level of intelligence than any journalist had till then explored. To interest the child mind he employed the old device of pictures, his favorite illustration portraying the Plunderbund. Now, persons who thought the cartoon of the Plunderbund looked like themselves, viewed the experiment with alarm. But Mr. Hearst was right. He proved to be as he said he was, "our greatest conservative force." The surest guardians of our morals and of our social order are precisely Mr. Hearst's readers, who learned the alphabet spelling out P-L-U-N-D-E-R-B-U-N-D. They watch keenly and with reprobation in Mr. Hearst's press our slightest divagations.

De Gourmont, writing of education, asks: "Is it necessary to cultivate at such pains in the minds of the young, hatred of what is new?" And he says it is done only because the teacher naturally hates everything that has come into the world since he won his diploma. But no; De Gourmont is mistaken. It is because we teach the young what it is socially beneficial that they should learn, having regard also for their aversion to novelty, to the bottle from any other than the accustomed hands.

And we find in the child mind--and foster it by education--"the will to believe," that great American virtue. It requires an immense "will to believe" to grow up in the family and in society, looking at the elders and at all that is established, and accepting all the information that mankind has slowly accumulated and which teachers patiently offer. If the young once doubted, once thought--but unfortunately they do not! Anyway, we do find in the child mind, which forms the non-senseorship, the "will to believe,"--of immense social utility.

Now, the "will to believe"--like teeth which decay if not used upon hard food, or muscles which grow flabby if they have not hard work to perform--must be given something for its proper exercise. In a chapter on "The Duty of Lying," in his brilliant book ***Disenchantment***, Mr. C. E. Montague shows what may be done with "the will to believe," developed as it has at last been. "During the war the art of Propaganda was little more than born." In the next war, "the whole sky would be darkened with flights of tactical lies, so dense that the enemy would fight in a veritable 'fog of war' darker than London's own November brews, and the world would feel that not only the Angel of Death was abroad, but the Angel of Delusion too, and would hear the beating of two pairs of wings." And what may be done with the "will to believe" in time of war has immense lessons for the days of peace. A British Tommy, quoted by Mr. Montague, summed the moral advantages up: "They tell me we've pulled through at last all right because our propergander dished up better lies than what the Germans did. So I say to myself: 'If tellin' lies is all that bloody good in war, what bloody good is tellin' truth in peace?'" What "bloody good" is it, when you have ready to hand the well-trained "will to believe," which those who censored reason for its social disutility set up as the most serviceable attribute of the human mind?

I think I have written enough to prove that the child mind at the bottom of nonsenseorship is the effective base of stability. But the heart of man desires also permanency. Is there reasonable assurance that we shall always be able to keep the guiding principles of our national life, the nonsenseorship, a child mind?

It is true that we have reached as far down, through our press and through our public men, to the levels of the low I. Q. as it is practicable to go, until we grant actual children and not merely mental children an even larger share than they now have in the forming of public opinion; for this is, as you know, "the age of the child."

And no great further advance is likely to be made in the mechanical means of uniting the whole 100,000,000 people of this country in a 24-hour a day, 365 days a year, mass meeting. The cheap newspaper, the moving picture, instant telegraphic bulletin going everywhere, the broadcasting wireless telephone, and the Ford car, have accomplished all that can be hoped toward giving the widely-scattered population the responsiveness of a mob.

But though perhaps we may never lower the I. Q. of the nonsenseorship, no further triumphs being possible in that direction, there is no reason why education, what we call "creating an enlightened public opinion," should not always maintain for us the child mind as it now is with all its manifold advantages.

Somewhere in Bartlett there is, or ought to be, a quotation which reads like this: "The god who always finds us young and always keeps us so." That is education; it always finds us young and always keeps us so.

It catches us when our minds are merely acquisitive, storing up impressions and information; and it prolongs that period of acquisition to maturity by always throwing facts in our way. Its purpose is not to "sow doubts," far from it, for that would have for its ideal mere intelligence and not social usefulness. It develops instead the "will to believe," and this serves the needs of the propagandists, who, as Mr. Will H. Hayes is reported to have said of the movies, "shake the rattle which keeps the American child amused so that it forgets its aches and pains." We may safely trust education to keep the American mind infantile, merely acquisitive and not critical. And thus the nonsenseorship seems sure to be perpetuated, and we reach the ideal of all the ages, society in its permanent and final form. Here we are, here we may rest.

These considerations persuade me at least that we should make the utmost sacrifices for so perfect a social means as we now have. Let the nonsenseorship invade the secret closets of our personality and rummage out our most cherished suppressed desires. Let us have nothing that we may call our own. For my part, I shall spend the proceeds of this article upon one of the new social police, a psycho-analyst.

### The Codes Of Hammurabi And Moses
### W. W. Davies

QTY

The discovery of the Hammurabi Code is one of the greatest achievements of archaeology, and is of paramount interest, not only to the student of the Bible, but also to all those interested in ancient history...

**Religion**     **ISBN:** *1-59462-338-4*          **Pages:132**
                                                    *MSRP $12.95*

### The Theory of Moral Sentiments
### Adam Smith

QTY

This work from 1749. contains original theories of conscience amd moral judgment and it is the foundation for systemof morals.

**Philosophy**  **ISBN:** *1-59462-777-0*          **Pages:536**
                                                    *MSRP $19.95*

### Jessica's First Prayer
### Hesba Stretton

QTY

In a screened and secluded corner of one of the many railway-bridges which span the streets of London there could be seen a few years ago, from five o'clock every morning until half past eight, a tidily set-out coffee-stall, consisting of a trestle and board, upon which stood two large tin cans, with a small fire of charcoal burning under each so as to keep the coffee boiling during the early hours of the morning when the work-people were thronging into the city on their way to their daily toil...

**Childrens**   **ISBN:** *1-59462-373-2*     **Pages:84**
                                              *MSRP $9.95*

### My Life and Work
### Henry Ford

QTY

Henry Ford revolutionized the world with his implementation of mass production for the Model T automobile. Gain valuable business insight into his life and work with his own auto-biography... "We have only started on our development of our country we have not as yet, with all our talk of wonderful progress, done more than scratch the surface. The progress has been wonderful enough but..."

**Biographies/**   **ISBN:** *1-59462-198-5*     **Pages:300**
                                                 *MSRP $21.95*

## The Art of Cross-Examination
## Francis Wellman

QTY

I presume it is the experience of every author, after his first book is published upon an important subject, to be almost overwhelmed with a wealth of ideas and illustrations which could readily have been included in his book, and which to his own mind, at least, seem to make a second edition inevitable. Such certainly was the case with me; and when the first edition had reached its sixth impression in five months, I rejoiced to learn that it seemed to my publishers that the book had met with a sufficiently favorable reception to justify a second and considerably enlarged edition. ..

**Pages:412**

**Reference    ISBN:** *1-59462-647-2*        *MSRP $19.95*

## On the Duty of Civil Disobedience
## Henry David Thoreau

QTY

Thoreau wrote his famous essay, On the Duty of Civil Disobedience, as a protest against an unjust but popular war and the immoral but popular institution of slave-owning. He did more than write—he declined to pay his taxes, and was hauled off to gaol in consequence. Who can say how much this refusal of his hastened the end of the war and of slavery ?

**Law          ISBN:** *1-59462-747-9*          **Pages:48**

*MSRP $7.45*

## Dream Psychology Psychoanalysis for Beginners
## Sigmund Freud

QTY

Sigmund Freud, born Sigismund Schlomo Freud (May 6, 1856 - September 23, 1939), was a Jewish-Austrian neurologist and psychiatrist who co-founded the psychoanalytic school of psychology. Freud is best known for his theories of the unconscious mind, especially involving the mechanism of repression; his redefinition of sexual desire as mobile and directed towards a wide variety of objects; and his therapeutic techniques, especially his understanding of transference in the therapeutic relationship and the presumed value of dreams as sources of insight into unconscious desires.

**Pages:196**

**Psychology    ISBN:** *1-59462-905-6*        *MSRP $15.45*

## The Miracle of Right Thought
## Orison Swett Marden

QTY

Believe with all of your heart that you will do what you were made to do. When the mind has once formed the habit of holding cheerful, happy, prosperous pictures, it will not be easy to form the opposite habit. It does not matter how improbable or how far away this realization may see, or how dark the prospects may be, if we visualize them as best we can, as vividly as possible, hold tenaciously to them and vigorously struggle to attain them, they will gradually become actualized, realized in the life. But a desire, a longing without endeavor, a yearning abandoned or held indifferently will vanish without realization.

**Pages:360**

**Self Help          ISBN:** *1-59462-644-8*      *MSRP $25.45*

QTY

**The Rosicrucian Cosmo-Conception Mystic Christianity** *by Max Heindel*    ISBN: *1-59462-188-8*    **$38.95**
*The Rosicrucian Cosmo-conception is not dogmatic, neither does it appeal to any other authority than the reason of the student. It is; not controversial, but is; sent forth in the, hope that it may help to clear..*    New Age/Religion Pages 646

**Abandonment To Divine Providence** *by Jean-Pierre de Caussade*    ISBN: *1-59462-228-0*    **$25.95**
*"The Rev. Jean Pierre de Caussade was one of the most remarkable spiritual writers of the Society of Jesus in France in the 18th Century. His death took place at Toulouse in 1751. His works have gone through many editions and have been republished...*    Inspirational/Religion Pages 400

**Mental Chemistry** *by Charles Haanel*    ISBN: *1-59462-192-6*    **$23.95**
*Mental Chemistry allows the change of material conditions by combining and appropriately utilizing the power of the mind. Much like applied chemistry creates something new and unique out of careful combinations of chemicals the mastery of mental chemistry...*    New Age Pages 354

**The Letters of Robert Browning and Elizabeth Barret Barrett 1845-1846 vol II**    ISBN: *1-59462-193-4*    **$35.95**
*by Robert Browning and Elizabeth Barrett*    Biographies Pages 596

**Gleanings In Genesis (volume I)** *by Arthur W. Pink*    ISBN: *1-59462-130-6*    **$27.45**
*Appropriately has Genesis been termed "the seed plot of the Bible" for in it we have, in germ form, almost all of the great doctrines which are afterwards fully developed in the books of Scripture which follow...*    Religion/Inspirational Pages 420

**The Master Key** *by L. W. de Laurence*    ISBN: *1-59462-001-6*    **$30.95**
*In no branch of human knowledge has there been a more lively increase of the spirit of research during the past few years than in the study of Psychology, Concentration and Mental Discipline. The requests for authentic lessons in Thought Control, Mental Discipline and...*    New Age/Business Pages 422

**The Lesser Key Of Solomon Goetia** *by L. W. de Laurence*    ISBN: *1-59462-092-X*    **$9.95**
*This translation of the first book of the "Lernegton" which is now for the first time made accessible to students of Talismanic Magic was done, after careful collation and edition, from numerous Ancient Manuscripts in Hebrew, Latin, and French...*    New Age/Occult Pages 92

**Rubaiyat Of Omar Khayyam** *by Edward Fitzgerald*    ISBN:*1-59462-332-5*    **$13.95**
*Edward Fitzgerald, whom the world has already learned, in spite of his own efforts to remain within the shadow of anonymity, to look upon as one of the rarest poets of the century, was born at Bredfield, in Suffolk, on the 31st of March, 1809. He was the third son of John Purcell...*    Music Pages 172

**Ancient Law** *by Henry Maine*    ISBN: *1-59462-128-4*    **$29.95**
*The chief object of the following pages is to indicate some of the earliest ideas of mankind, as they are reflected in Ancient Law, and to point out the relation of those ideas to modern thought.*    Religion/History Pages 452

**Far-Away Stories** *by William J. Locke*    ISBN: *1-59462-129-2*    **$19.45**
*"Good wine needs no bush, but a collection of mixed vintages does. And this book is just such a collection. Some of the stories I do not want to remain buried for ever in the museum files of dead magazine-numbers an author's not unpardonable vanity..."*    Fiction Pages 272

**Life of David Crockett** *by David Crockett*    ISBN: *1-59462-250-7*    **$27.45**
*"Colonel David Crockett was one of the most remarkable men of the times in which he lived. Born in humble life, but gifted with a strong will, an indomitable courage, and unremitting perseverance...*    Biographies/New Age Pages 424

**Lip-Reading** *by Edward Nitchie*    ISBN: *1-59462-206-X*    **$25.95**
*Edward B. Nitchie, founder of the New York School for the Hard of Hearing, now the Nitchie School of Lip-Reading, Inc, wrote "LIP-READING Principles and Practice". The development and perfecting of this meritorious work on lip-reading was an undertaking...*    How-to Pages 400

**A Handbook of Suggestive Therapeutics, Applied Hypnotism, Psychic Science**    ISBN: *1-59462-214-0*    **$24.95**
*by Henry Munro*    Health/New Age/Health/Self-help Pages 376

**A Doll's House: and Two Other Plays** *by Henrik Ibsen*    ISBN: *1-59462-112-8*    **$19.95**
*Henrik Ibsen created this classic when in revolutionary 1848 Rome. Introducing some striking concepts in playwriting for the realist genre, this play has been studied the world over.*    Fiction/Classics/Plays 308

**The Light of Asia** *by sir Edwin Arnold*    ISBN: *1-59462-204-3*    **$13.95**
*In this poetic masterpiece, Edwin Arnold describes the life and teachings of Buddha. The man who was to become known as Buddha to the world was born as Prince Gautama of India but he rejected the worldly riches and abandoned the reigns of power when...*    Religion/History/Biographies Pages 170

**The Complete Works of Guy de Maupassant** *by Guy de Maupassant*    ISBN: *1-59462-157-8*    **$16.95**
*"For days and days, nights and nights, I had dreamed of that first kiss which was to consecrate our engagement, and I knew not on what spot I should put my lips..."*    Fiction/Classics Pages 240

**The Art of Cross-Examination** *by Francis L. Wellman*    ISBN: *1-59462-309-0*    **$26.95**
*Written by a renowned trial lawyer, Wellman imparts his experience and uses case studies to explain how to use psychology to extract desired information through questioning.*    How-to/Science/Reference Pages 408

**Answered or Unanswered?** *by Louisa Vaughan*    ISBN: *1-59462-248-5*    **$10.95**
*Miracles of Faith in China*    Religion Pages 112

**The Edinburgh Lectures on Mental Science (1909)** *by Thomas*    ISBN: *1-59462-008-3*    **$11.95**
*This book contains the substance of a course of lectures recently given by the writer in the Queen Street Hall, Edinburgh. Its purpose is to indicate the Natural Principles governing the relation between Mental Action and Material Conditions...*    New Age/Psychology Pages 148

**Ayesha** *by H. Rider Haggard*    ISBN: *1-59462-301-5*    **$24.95**
*Verily and indeed it is the unexpected that happens! Probably if there was one person upon the earth from whom the Editor of this, and of a certain previous history, did not expect to hear again...*    Classics Pages 380

**Ayala's Angel** *by Anthony Trollope*    ISBN: *1-59462-352-X*    **$29.95**
*The two girls were both pretty, but Lucy who was twenty-one who supposed to be simple and comparatively unattractive, whereas Ayala was credited, as her Bombwhat romantic name might show, with poetic charm and a taste for romance. Ayala when her father died was nineteen...*    Fiction Pages 484

**The American Commonwealth** *by James Bryce*    ISBN: *1-59462-286-8*    **$34.45**
*An interpretation of American democratic political theory. It examines political mechanics and society from the perspective of Scotsman James Bryce*    Politics Pages 572

**Stories of the Pilgrims** *by Margaret P. Pumphrey*    ISBN: *1-59462-116-0*    **$17.95**
*This book explores pilgrims religious oppression in England as well as their escape to Holland and eventual crossing to America on the Mayflower, and their early days in New England...*    History Pages 268

QTY

**The Fasting Cure** *by Sinclair Upton*　　　　　　　　　ISBN: *1-59462-222-1*　**$13.95**
*In the Cosmopolitan Magazine for May, 1910, and in the Contemporary Review (London) for April, 1910, I published an article dealing with my experiences in fasting. I have written a great many magazine articles, but never one which attracted so much attention... New Age/Self Help/Health Pages 164*

**Hebrew Astrology** *by Sepharial*　　　　　　　　　ISBN: *1-59462-308-2*　**$13.45**
*In these days of advanced thinking it is a matter of common observation that we have left many of the old landmarks behind and that we are now pressing forward to greater heights and to a wider horizon than that which represented the mind-content of our progenitors...　Astrology Pages 144*

**Thought Vibration or The Law of Attraction in the Thought World**　　ISBN: *1-59462-127-6*　**$12.95**
*by William Walker Atkinson*　　　　　　　　　　　　　*Psychology/Religion Pages 144*

**Optimism** *by Helen Keller*　　　　　　　　　　ISBN: *1-59462-108-X*　**$15.95**
*Helen Keller was blind, deaf, and mute since 19 months old, yet famously learned how to overcome these handicaps, communicate with the world, and spread her lectures promoting optimism. An inspiring read for everyone...　Biographies/Inspirational Pages 84*

**Sara Crewe** *by Frances Burnett*　　　　　　　　　ISBN: *1-59462-360-0*　**$9.45**
*In the first place, Miss Minchin lived in London. Her home was a large, dull, tall one, in a large, dull square, where all the houses were alike, and all the sparrows were alike, and where all the door-knockers made the same heavy sound...　Childrens/Classic Pages 88*

**The Autobiography of Benjamin Franklin** *by Benjamin Franklin*　　ISBN: *1-59462-135-7*　**$24.95**
*The Autobiography of Benjamin Franklin has probably been more extensively read than any other American historical work, and no other book of its kind has had such ups and downs of fortune. Franklin lived for many years in England, where he was agent...　Biographies/History Pages 332*

| | |
|---|---|
| **Name** | |
| **Email** | |
| **Telephone** | |
| **Address** | |
| | |
| **City, State ZIP** | |

☐ **Credit Card**　　　　　☐ **Check / Money Order**

| | |
|---|---|
| **Credit Card Number** | |
| **Expiration Date** | |
| **Signature** | |

*Please Mail to:　Book Jungle*
*PO Box 2226*
*Champaign, IL 61825*
*or Fax to:　　　630-214-0564*

## ORDERING INFORMATION

**web**: *www.bookjungle.com*
**email**: *sales@bookjungle.com*
**fax**: *630-214-0564*
**mail**: *Book Jungle  PO Box 2226  Champaign, IL 61825*
**or PayPal** *to sales@bookjungle.com*

*Please contact us for bulk discounts*

## DIRECT-ORDER TERMS

**20% Discount if You Order
Two or More Books**
Free Domestic Shipping!
Accepted: Master Card, Visa,
Discover, American Express